D1359074

MistOver MorroBay

CAROLE GIFT PAGE/DORIS ELAINE FELL

HARVEST HOUSE PUBLISHERS
Eugene, OR 97402

All persons and groups of persons mentioned in this book are fictional; any resemblance to actual persons or groups of persons is purely coincidental.

MIST OVER MORRO BAY

Copyright © 1985 by Carole Gift Page and
Doris Elaine Fell
Published by Harvest House Publishers
Eugene, Oregon 97402

ISBN 0-89081-462-7

Printed in the United States of America.

To Sheila Cragg,
who began this quixotic journey with us,
shared in the vision for this book,
and gave so freely of her writing
and editorial skills:
our love and our thanks.

And in loving memory of
Julie Lynne Fell
—22 years old—
Sensitive, gentle-spirited
and fragile-winged

Mist Over Morro Bay

CHAPTER ONE

"Are you nervous about flying, Miss Merrill?" asked David Ballard with a solicitation that made me bristle.

"Nervous? No, not at all, Mr. Ballard," I replied, tossing my hair jauntily. Still, as our Beechcraft Bonanza bounced about in the October winds, my stomach churned. I felt as if I were in a glass bubble that might shatter momentarily. "Flying in a small plane is a little bumpier than I expected," I said, my voice wavering.

"Clouds," he told me.

"What?"

7

"Turbulence. Clouds make turbulence."

"Yes, of course." I stole a peeved glance his way. How ignorant did he think I was?

Since our takeoff from Orange County Airport I had sat in tense silence in the copilot seat watching as my employer squinted owlishly over the Bonanza's complex instrument panel. His ease and skillfulness as he worked the controls bespoke years of experience, but his attitude this morning was aloof and condescending. He reminded me of a doctor with a rotten bedside manner.

I knew I wasn't his first choice for this trip. He wanted his devoted Eva, but a sudden attack of flu changed her plans, and I was her last-minute replacement. I had a feeling that Mr. Ballard wasn't about to forgive me for taking her place.

"Michelle," he said, "you realize the Bonanza's not like flying in a 747 or a DC-10."

"You're telling me. No one's even offered me a mint or a magazine."

My feeble attempt at humor failed to alleviate my queasiness. It wasn't supposed to be like this—an important business trip to San Jose with the firm's owner in his company plane. I had imagined myself being the envy of all the girls in the office. David Ballard was the talk of the powder room—a handsome, eligible bachelor, wealthy and sophisticated, a rare mixture of charm and mystery. He was a private person who wasn't given to casual chitchat, which only made him more alluring to the secretarial pool.

In my six months at Ballard Computer Design, I had considered myself above the starry-eyed girls who dreamed of being swept off their feet by Mr. Ballard. I had already been hurt once by a man; I wasn't about to make the same mistake again.

As if to confirm my resolution afresh, I gazed appraisingly at David now. He was staring straight ahead. A lean, muscular man with a coppery complexion, he had chestnut hair and a long, slightly irregular nose. He had the shadow of a beard except where a faint scar traced the cleft of his chin and ran along his square jawline. He was wearing a jade-green rugby shirt, khaki slacks, and penny loafers, a far cry from his usual business gray. Reluctantly, I had to admit he was an attractive man.

What could possibly provide more fuel for my writer's imagination, I wondered, than flying alone with the stubborn, virile, unfathomable David Ballard? Think of the descriptive passages I could scribble in my pocket notebook from 10,000 feet. *The two of us together in his sleek Bonanza . . . climbing . . . cutting through cream . . . exhilarating!* Except that now, if I looked down past the white, blue-tipped wing, I'd lose more than I would gain—my breakfast, at least.

I stared instead at the illuminated instrument panel with its myriad dials and made another stab at conversation. "So many gadgets, Mr. Ballard. I'm amazed at how you keep them all straight."

He gave me a terse, "It comes from my experience as a Navy pilot." Gesturing toward the controls directly in front of me, he added, "There's the radio. You can put on the extra headset and listen in to the air traffic if you like."

"I don't care to listen to the radio," I told him pointedly. Why did he have to be so surly when I just wanted to be sociable?

"Well, we don't offer the latest full-length feature on this flight, Miss Merrill."

"I didn't expect to be entertained, Mr. Ballard."

"I would think not. This *is* a business trip, you know." He paused. "Actually, I'm afraid it's business you know very little about."

My anger was suddenly white hot. *The arrogant boar!* "Mr. Ballard, I know I'm not Eva. I know you wanted her to make this trip with you, but please don't take your irritation out on me. I've been with Ballard Computer Design only six months, but I plan to do my best for the company."

He looked at me, startled. "What are you talking about?"

"You've been so sullen. You've hardly said a civil word the whole trip."

"I've had my mind on this business deal." He hesitated. "And I was counting on Eva's expertise. She worked on this transaction from the beginning. If everything goes well, I'll be signing one of our most important contracts this afternoon."

"Can't you sign it without Eva?"

David's dark eyes crinkled with a rare smile. "Eva's been with me since I started the company. She's more than a secretary. She's my right arm."

"It sounds like she's even more than that."

"She is. She was the mother of my best friend."

I caught my breath in surprise. "I never knew Eva had a child. I always thought she was a spinster."

"No—a widow. Her son, Rob Thornton, was my bombardier-navigator in Vietnam."

"Eva never mentioned him to me."

The muscle under David's right eye twitched slightly. "He's dead."

Suddenly I felt like a blundering idiot. "Oh, I'm sorry." I looked out the window at the gray, gathering clouds.

"Well, it was a long time ago."

I turned back to David. "What happened?"

He ground his jaw stonily. There was a raw intensity in his expression as he said, "I was with Rob. We were flying a mission north of Hanoi when our plane was hit by enemy fire. We limped along until we found a small clearing and crash-landed. We both made it out of the plane alive, but Rob was killed moments later by an exploding grenade. The explosion knocked me nearly to kingdom come and tore open my face." He touched his scar with a tapered finger. "I woke up days later in a remote helicopter base south of the DMZ. I was lucky our guys found me and not the North Vietnamese." His coal-hard eyes softened to a slate gray. "Not luck," he corrected. "I don't believe in luck. It was a miracle."

"It was a nightmare," I murmured.

"That too." David gazed frankly at me. "People I know usually don't hear this story. I reserve it for strangers on airplanes . . . and attractive secretaries," he added with a hint of lightness.

"I appreciate your sharing something so painful with me."

He shrugged. "I don't know why I did. Maybe to make amends for my rudeness, for taking out my frustration over Eva on you. I didn't realize my lousy mood was showing." He flashed me an apologetic smile. "I bet you had to cancel important plans of your own to accompany me on this trip."

I nodded. "I'm afraid so. I was supposed to be at Sebastian's tonight for dinner and a play."

He lifted one eyebrow quizzically. "Oh, a heavy date?"

"That would be telling," I teased. I didn't add

that I was going with three girls from the office.

"What's playing?"

"Funny Girl." I sighed wistfully. "I sure did want to see that musical."

"Tell you what. When we get back from San Jose, I'll take you myself. It'll be my treat."

"I'd like that. In fact, they have a Sunday brunch, if you're interested."

He shook his head. "It'll have to be some evening. Sundays are really full for me. I teach a Sunday school class of junior high boys and sponsor the youth fellowship after the evening service."

"You're a glutton for punishment," I remarked. Privately, I couldn't picture the great David Ballard coping with rowdy, boisterous, gum-chewing adolescents. "How did you get roped into all of that?"

He chuckled. "Believe it or not, I volunteered. Serving God was one of my Vietnam commitments. Besides, my own teenage years were the loneliest of my life. I want these kids to know that God is the answer to their loneliness."

I knew what David was talking about, but lately religion wasn't my favorite topic. I purposely changed the subject. "If Sundays are out, perhaps we should plan on Saturday night for 'Funny Girl,' Mr. Ballard."

"Call me David," he said. "You've earned the right, listening with such patience to my mordant tales and coming away with me when you had better plans. I can't promise sweetness and light for the rest of the trip, but I'll try my hand at a soggy joke or two." He offered a wide, generous grin. "Who knows? I might even make you laugh."

"That isn't necessary, Mr. Bal—David."

"When I telephone Eva tonight, I'll have her

make reservations at Sebastian's for us."

"You're going to call her even when she's home sick?"

"Frankly, she's used to my eccentric ways, my constantly relying on her. She's a mother figure and a saint in one compact little woman," remarked David. He wasn't kidding.

"I never would have guessed she lost a son," I responded. "She's always so cheerful, so positive."

"I learned a great deal from the way she handled Rob's death."

"Tell me, David, how did the two of you get together? Did you know Eva before Vietnam?"

"No, except through her reams of letters and dog-eared photographs that Rob carried around. He was a bright, bashful guy, dependable as the sunrise, and he doted on his mother. Didn't care who knew it, either. He made me promise to look her up if anything ever happened to him."

"You promised without even knowing her?" David Ballard was rising in my estimation by the minute.

"Why not? Once I met her, I practically adopted her. My own mother died when I was ten, Dad when I was 20. I was a late, only child. After Rob was killed, I figured Eva and I needed each other. She was already a crack secretary when I started my company. Over the years she's become one of the best businesswomen I know. More important, she's a loyal friend."

"I'm beginning to understand your disappointment over her absence today."

"It wasn't personal, Michelle," David assured me. "In fact, at the moment it feels....downright providential."

CHAPTER
TWO

The Bonanza banked to the right. "Look, Michelle, there's a slight break in the overcast. Santa Barbara's below us."

I followed David's gaze. Highway 101 stretched below like a strand of spaghetti; fog marbled the coastline. The rolling landscape was a nauseating green.

I looked away. I had to admit that I hated heights. "Oh, Shakespeare!" I uttered under my breath.

"What?" David queried.

I pretended not to hear him.

He persisted. "You mentioned. . . Shakespeare?"

I blushed in spite of myself. "I said, 'Oh, Shake-speare.' We said that in college whenever something went wrong. You know, a harmless expletive. I majored in English lit."

"I see," said David. He paused. "Then how did you happen to become a secretary and not a teacher?"

"Actually, I hadn't planned to become either one. I'd like to earn my living as a writer."

"Write? You mean . . . books?" He sounded incredulous.

"Yes. Someday. Who knows? I might even write the Great American Novel."

"I think that's marvelous," he said, his dark eyes crinkling merrily. Was he jesting? "Have you been published?" he inquired.

"A few times. Short stories mainly." I tried to quell the enthusiasm that always bubbles when I talk about my writing. "In little magazines," I added. "Nothing you would have heard of."

"Try me," he said lightly. "I majored in business administration, but English was my minor. I still read Cheever or Melville on occasion."

"Really? How do you find the time?"

He chuckled. "In spite of the impression you may have, Michelle, I don't spend all of my time with computers."

I flushed slightly. "I didn't mean it that way, David."

"I know." He looked over and smiled. "As a writer, you must be looking forward to our trip to Blair Publishers today." He advanced the throttle and scanned the instrument panel routinely. "One of my reps has already sold Blair on my computer design program. I just have a few terms to finalize before we sign the contract. Your duties are simple. Just take notes. Eva likes detail."

I hesitated. "Does this business deal involve computer hardware, software, or both?"

"Strictly software," he answered. "It's a million-dollar computer program for Blair and its magazine conglomerate."

Reflectively I twisted a strand of my burnished hair. "Doesn't Blair publish the airline magazine?"

"Yes, the smaller airlines, like Midwest Airways."

"I thought so. I sold them an article about the Chicago Loop several years ago."

David whistled. "I'm impressed."

I laughed. "So was I. It was my first sale after a season of rejections."

"So you know all about rejections?"

I flinched, thinking suddenly and involuntarily of Scott—the love of my life, the bane of my soul. "I know enough about rejection to last a lifetime," I answered grimly, my mood suddenly as dark as the gathering rain clouds that enveloped our plane.

David glanced over, curious. "Are we still talking about magazines?"

I stared out the windshield. "What else is there?" I bit my lip at the flippancy of my reply.

David's tone assumed a pleasant formality, drawing me back. "So how did you happen to write about Chicago?"

"I grew up in Lake Forest and graduated from Hopewell."

"Oh, I know Hopewell Christian College. I had some Navy buddies who graduated from there. They bragged about its excellent scholastic standards."

"And its loads of rules and regulations?"

"Yeah, they had a few choice remarks about those

too. Were you one of those venturesome people constantly on the verge of being shipped?"

"I did rake up enough demerits to be campused one semester."

"Come now. What dastardly deeds did you commit?"

"I wrote poems after bed check with a flashlight under my pillow. I skipped devotions a few times. And then one weekend during my senior year my boyfriend Scott came for the homecoming basketball game. He walked me home afterward, and as we approached my dormitory, I spied the dorm monitor on patrol. When Scott started to kiss me good night, I protested, reminding him of the strict rules: no kissing or hand-holding, or I'd be out bag and baggage. He grinned mischievously, grabbed me, and kissed me soundly. When I looked up at the monitor—this hefty girl with stumpy legs and a granite expression—I knew my days at Hopewell were numbered. She marched up to Scott in her navy pleated skirt and high-necked blouse and demanded his name. With the gallantry of Sir Walter Raleigh, he took her thick hand and kissed it with a flourish. She was so flustered she turned and bustled off to find the house mother."

"And you weren't expelled for that escapade?"

"No, just campused for the rest of the semester. My hall monitor, Jill Monroe, a girl I once considered my friend, had to escort me all over campus. I was literally under guard. Jill accompanied me to meals in the dining common and sat with me in chapel. I wasn't allowed to speak to boys, date, or see Scott. Of course, I got around that on weekends when I went home. But the whole experience was demeaning. I felt like an untouchable."

"Why did you stay there?"

"My parents wanted me to graduate from Hopewell. Actually I did, too. I wouldn't trade the education I received there for anything. The English professors were outstanding. My journalism instructor gave me my first real encouragement to pursue writing as a career. Of course that irritated my dad. He wanted me to major in business instead of English and someday take over the family drugstore."

"Your father's a pharmacist?"

"No, he's the owner-manager of Andrew's Apothecary, a quaint little store with one of the old-fashioned soda fountains where you can still get an authentic chocolate malt or a cherry Coke. I used to work there summers and after school. I was forever getting into trouble for reading the paperbacks. Those were my glory days—sitting in a corner with Agatha Christie or Phyllis Whitney, devouring Baby Ruths. Sometimes I sat at the counter and jotted down descriptions of the customers on paper napkins to use in my stories. My younger sister Pam always scowled disapprovingly at me while she scooped mounds of rocky road ice cream for the grimy, barefoot neighborhood kids who banged in and out through our noisy screen door. But I couldn't imagine a lifetime of dishing up hot fudge sundaes, wiping counters, and ringing a cash register. So after graduation from Hopewell, I got a job for about a year with a small, local publishing company as a first reader, wading through their slush pile of unsolicited manuscripts."

"So how did you find your way to California?" asked David.

"In my little brown Honda. It was my graduation

present." I didn't add that I'd driven alone and cried all the way.

"That's *how* you got here, but you didn't tell me *why*. Surely you didn't come out here just to work for Ballard Computer Design Corporation."

"Of course," I said with a frivolousness I didn't feel. I shifted uneasily, reflecting, *You would have run away too if your fiance had eloped with one of your best friends two weeks before your wedding!* Aloud I continued, "Being a first reader didn't open any doors to staff writing. So I decided to come out to Morro Bay to be near Jackie, my college roommate. But I heard there were more opportunities in Orange County."

"For writers?"

"For jobs. Freelance writing doesn't even put macaroni and cheese on the table."

Before David could respond, there was a burst of smoke from the nose of the Bonanza. The plane lurched. Its engine coughed and sputtered.

I stiffened. The hum of the motor was gone!

David tightened his hands on the controls. His eyes scanned the oil pressure gauge. The needle was plummeting. The propeller momentum fluttered. He checked the fuel gauges and the altimeter.

"What's wrong?" I asked with alarm.

"We've lost power. But don't worry. I've turned on the auxiliary fuel pump and switched to the reserve gas tank."

I stared transfixed at the control panel at what appeared to be a miniature TV screen. The image of a plane flip-flopped crazily. "Is that us?" I cried.

David ignored me. The propeller was windmilling. The engine turned over, droned momentarily, then stalled again. He clenched his jaw as he pressed his microphone button to transmit. "Santa Maria tower, this is Bonanza N35DB. My engine's gone. I'm losing altitude. Over."

The controller's voice was crisp. "We read you, Bonanza N35DB. Where are you?"

"Five miles from Lompoc."

"Can you make it to Santa Maria?"

"Negative."

"Are you declaring an emergency?"

"Yes. We're losing altitude rapidly."

"Then Lompoc is your best bet," returned the controller. "Stand by for instructions."

"Stand by?" My voice rose precariously. "Without an engine?"

"I've faced worse landings than this in Nam." David's voice was husky. "I'll get us down, Michelle."

"But—where?"

The controller cut in with, "Lompoc reports weather closing in . . . gusty winds . . . visibility down. Advise landing at Meadowgreen."

"Roger," replied David. With a flick of his wrist he adjusted the radio frequency to 121.8. "Meadowgreen Airport, this is Bonanza N35DB. Requesting emergency clearance . . . I have no power . . . I'm coming in on a deadstick landing . . . runway one-seven."

I felt my throat constricting. "Meadowgreen sounds like a cow pasture!"

Beads of sweat stood out on David's forehead. Still, he winked at me as he gestured toward the narrow strip of wet blacktop in the distance. "It's okay," he said. "No cows."

Seconds later he banked over the field and came in at a southwesterly approach. The clouds were

darkening ominously and spitting enormous drops
on the windshield. The plane veered as David made
a futile attempt to release the retractable gear. Then
he reached behind him to his right, gripped a lever,
and cranked it with a fierceness that made me
shudder.

"What are you doing?" I cried, hysteria in my
voice. "Aren't we going to land?"

David's words broke with raw tension. "We
will—if I can get these wheels down!"

"David, no!" I screamed. "We're going to crash!"

"Hold on tight," he warned. "We're committed
now. There's no go-around."

CHAPTER
THREE

The wind whistled eerily across the wings as the stalled Bonanza dipped earthward. We were riding the wind down, breaking through a shroud of gray mist. I gritted my teeth and gripped the leather armrest, my knuckles bone-white as waves of panic swept over me. My eyes were riveted on the narrow black strip rising to meet us.

The dollhouse images of trees and barns were mushrooming dizzily. I felt like Alice in Wonderland being sucked down the rabbit hole, a pounding pressure in my head, my feet braced for a landing, the land jumping up crazily to meet me—trees and grass. . .blind panic. . .hypnotizing.

Oh, God, I'm scared! I haven't talked to You for so long—

There was a click. The plane bounced as the landing gear locked down. "The wheels are in place," David told me. He was breathing hard.

The back wheels hit first, skidding, bumping over the blacktop, rubber peeling against pavement. The nose touched down jarringly; then the lean aircraft leapfrogged over the airfield. I pitched forward. My seatbelt cut across my abdomen, painfully tight. My pulse raced. I went blank with terror.

The plane shimmied along the glistening asphalt runway. Vapors of steam swallowed us, then cleared. A Cessna beside the hangar blurred, sweeping phantomlike in and out of view. The Bonanza vibrated as it strained against the brakes, its wheels shrieking in protest. The aircraft squealed to a shuddering stop, swerving at the edge of the runway.

"Thank God!" said David, sinking back against the cushioned backrest. His hands still gripped the controls.

I stared dazed out the cockpit window at the motionless propeller. Relief washed over me. I looked at David and tried to summon a smile. "You—I—we—" I began. Then suddenly, unexpectedly, the tears came. I buried my face in my hands and wept.

David put an awkward, comforting arm around my shoulder and gave me his handkerchief. While I dabbed my eyes, he unbuckled our seatbelts and reached across me to open the door.

"We're going to get out, Michelle," he said, "but you'll have to turn sideways, step up on the seat, and climb out onto the wing."

"I—I can't. I'm shaking so badly."

"You'll be okay. I'll be right behind you. I'll help you down."

Clutching my canvas shoulder bag, I stepped gingerly onto the slippery wing. David followed, supporting me with a firm hand. Then he slipped past me and climbed down onto a narrow step below the wing. Once on the ground, he reached up and lifted me down with strong arms.

A spasm of shivers went through my body as my feet touched the earth. I swayed; everything was going black around me. Suddenly I felt myself being gathered up into David's arms.

"Are you all right?" he asked. The rain made beads in his tousled hair.

I rested my head against his chest. "I'm fine now. My legs just felt a little wobbly."

"You'll feel better as soon as we get inside, dry off, and have some coffee."

"It's a miracle you got us down, David."

"No, Michelle, it wasn't *my* miracle."

Before I could reply, there was a shout from the hangar. A squat, bullish man in a gray sweatshirt and tilted visor cap came galumphing through the rain toward us. "Hey, you folks okay? When I heard that engine cutting out I figured you was going to land on your belly!" As he approached, he wiped his thick hands on a red grease rag.

"You got a good mechanic here?" said David.

"You're looking at him. Clarence Harvey's the name." He stuck out a grimy paw. "I'm the owner, manager, and jack-of-all-trades of this ritzy establishment." He guffawed, his black eyes crinkling in his puffy face.

David extended his hand. "You ever repair a Bonanza?"

"Whenever one drops in on me like this."

"How soon can you get to my plane? I've got problems with my engine and I know for sure the vacuum pump's out."

"I can't have it for you yesterday, buddy." Clarence's craggy brows knit together. He spoke through clenched teeth. "It'll take several days. Weekend's coming up, you know. And I'll have to order the parts."

"Well, I've got an urgent appointment in San Jose this afternoon."

"Make that *next* Wednesday, buddy, and you'll be on time," snorted Clarence.

I looked up at David. His neck vein pulsated. Rain streaked his forehead and ran down along his scar to his cleft chin. I tugged at his arm. "David, we're getting soaked!"

Clarence made an exaggerated, sweeping gesture toward the nondescript airport cafe with its tilted sign, "Harvey's Hangar." "You'd better get the little lady inside. Run along and I'll start checking your aircraft over."

Inside the cafe, sitting in a small corner booth, I felt as if I would never stop trembling. I cupped my coffee mug, savoring the warmth. David reached across the table and rubbed my cold arms.

"I haven't had a close call like that since my crash landing in Vietnam," he told me, taking my hand. "Are you okay?"

"I'll be fine once I eat."

"Well, let's just hope the soup's good."

"I don't care if it's good as long as it's hot," I returned, teeth chattering. I surveyed our dreary surroundings. The garish green walls were plastered with sun-bleached flying posters. An antique propeller hung above the double doors and a six-foot, silver-blue sailfish arched over the bank of windows.

"Is the coffee helping?" asked David.

"I don't feel quite so numb now."

"Well, as soon as the proprietor of this classy dive gives me the word on my plane, I'll make other flight arrangements for San Jose," he said, his voice back to business. He checked his watch, then added, "Maybe we can still make it by three o'clock."

He glanced up as a heavy-hipped blonde in a miniskirt strutted toward us balancing a coffeepot and two tureens of soup. The liquid sloshed over the sides of the bowls as she slapped them on the table. "Homemade," she said, cracking her wad of gum.

I looked doubtfully at the soup, then smiled with amusement as David watched the waitress sashay away.

"Not bad," I said.

"What—the soup?"

"No, our charming waitress."

"Not my type." David dipped his spoon into his tureen. "Unlike this place, the soup is great."

"Just where is *this place*?"

"You mean Meadowgreen Airport?"

I nodded.

"We're about 30 miles south of Santa Maria."

I brightened. "Is that anywhere near Morro Bay?"

"About 70 miles south. Why?"

"My friend Jackie lives there."

"Oh, yes, your former college roommate."

"You remembered."

He tapped his temple lightly. "Computer-brain, you know."

I laughed. "No wonder everyone calls you Mr. Computer!"

"I've heard a rumor to that effect," he replied with a chuckle.

"I think I've just given away a company secret."

"No, I really don't mind being tagged 'Mr. Computer.' But I didn't compute what your friend is doing in Morro Bay."

"She lives there with her husband, Steve Turman, and their little boy. I haven't seen Jackie since our sophomore days, four years ago. What a carefree, happy-go-lucky year that was. And what scatter-brains *we* were!"

David grinned. "I bet you left your mark one way or another."

I stifled a laugh. "We did. Jackie and I will always be remembered as the Popcorn Pranksters of Hopewell."

"How did you earn that dubious title?" David quizzed.

"Well, there was this girl who needed money to stay in school. Jackie and I wanted to help her, so we decided to raise money by selling popcorn."

"Popcorn?" echoed David.

"It strikes me as a dumb idea now too, but as dormitory students our options were limited."

"So did it work?"

"Not the way we planned. Jackie and I bought jars and jars of popcorn and little white sacks to bag it in. We figured we'd peddle the stuff from room to room. During study hours college girls are the hungriest people on earth. The problem was, the only popcorn popper was in the laundry room. I forgot the seasoning salt, so I told Jackie to start the corn while I ran back to our room. When I returned, popcorn was billowing uncontrollably over the top of the popper. It rolled off the table onto the floor and unpopped kernels shot through the air like bullets. By the time I pulled the plug on the popper, the laundry room looked like White Christmas and smelled like Ringling Bros. Circus. Weeks later, girls were still finding popcorn in their clean clothes. Needless to say, we were banished from exercising our culinary skills in the laundry room."

"Evidently Jackie used too much popcorn," laughed David.

"That's an understatement," I replied. "She had poured in the entire jar. She was too ashamed to admit to me that, having come from a wealthy family, she didn't know the first thing about cooking."

"A true neophyte!" observed David.

"But she vowed she'd never get caught like that again. Now she boasts that she's quite a gourmet cook."

"What happened to the needy student?"

"Jackie paid the girl's tuition bill anonymously with the spending money her folks sent her. For two months we both lived off my paltry allowance."

"So, a noble ending after all!" He pushed his empty

soup tureen aside. "I imagine you two gals still reminisce about those days."

"Not lately," I admitted. "We used to write all the time, but Jackie's letters have dwindled in the last year. I suppose Stevie Junior keeps her busy now." I nibbled a cracker. "I sure wish I could see her again."

"Not this trip, I'm afraid." David drained his coffee cup and slid out of the booth. "But you could give her a call before we leave."

"Are we going now?"

"Do you mind? The rain has let up, but the fog is really rolling in. I want to check on my plane and see what problems our friend Clarence has uncovered."

David paid the check and we left the dingy cafe, edging our way under the building eaves to the sprawling galvanized hangar. David slid the door open and stepped aside so I could enter. The enormous hangar was dank and cold. Shelf upon shelf of airplane parts lined one wall. A row of high, muted windows cast narrow slats of light in eerie patterns across the room.

My high heels clicked noisily on the cement floor. David's hand touched my elbow as we passed drill presses, a tow vehicle, and a partly assembled antique biplane.

From one corner of the hangar, angry voices erupted. I recognized Clarence Harvey's homespun drawl as he insisted, "I told you, there'll be no more flights out today."

Two men stood by the counter facing the blustery manager. One was tall and slender in a stylish double-breasted raincoat. He had an elongated face with sun-bleached brows over deep-set eyes. A muscle in his cheek twitched slightly as he looked at his comrade and said, "Okay, Royce, get us out of this one."

Royce was thirtyish, an athletic, sullen-faced man with blond, blow-dried hair and an insolent pout. He wore an open sport shirt, cowhide leather jacket, and tight designer jeans. His hands were thrust deep in his pockets as he stepped toward Clarence and growled, "I said I'll take the plane up fog or no fog!"

"No plane, no way," Clarence shot back.

"We have to fly out of here today!" Royce persisted.

Clarence dismissed him with a contemptuous thrust of his hand. "Tell it to the weatherman! I'm not gonna take a chance with one of my planes in this pea soup!"

As David nudged me toward the angry threesome, I whispered, "I don't think we should interrupt Clarence now."

"He said no more flights today," David replied without slacking his pace. "We'd better listen in."

Royce raised his fist threateningly. "I warn you, Clarence, don't interfere in this. You know my passenger here, Paul—Mr. Mangano—has an urgent appointment in Denver."

Lowering his voice, Clarence said emphatically, "Royce, I told you I have everything taken care of. I'll get you out of here."

Paul Mangano pivoted sharply and stalked away from the counter. His eyes smoldered as he brushed past David. He clipped my shoulder, knocking me off balance, and strode on without a backward glance.

David reached out to steady me, then called after

the man, "Watch where you're going, fella! You almost knocked her over." David turned to me. "Are you all right?"

I rubbed my shoulder and neck. "He's a real gentleman," I said sarcastically. I stepped back and felt something hard under my foot. Leaning down, I retrieved a gold-engraved medallion with a single key. I held it up to David. "Looks like our friend dropped this."

Royce stepped forward and looked intently at me. His silver-blue eyes flashed black and bullet-sharp. "What you got there, miss?"

"A key ring someone dropped."

"It must be mine." He reached for the ring.

I held it back and examined it more closely. "The initials say P.M."

Royce looked stunned. A nervous tic in his left eye winked involuntarily. "P.M.?" he said. "Well, that— that's Mr. Mangano's." He thrust out his hand and grabbed for the key ring. "I'll take it and give it to him. He's coming right back."

I wrapped my fingers around the medallion and turned away in a huff. "That's all right. I'll give the key to your Mr. Mangano—and a piece of my mind while I'm at it."

David said with amusement, "You have your chance. Mr. Mangano is coming back right now."

I walked briskly, with chin high, toward the sober, sandy-haired man in the raincoat. I met him by the workbench, some distance from David and Royce, and dangled the key ring on my finger. "Mr. Mangano, I believe you dropped this when you nearly knocked me down a few minutes ago." My anger dissipated as I met the man's troubled gaze. His slender, handsome face appeared haggard. The dark creases beneath his eyes suggested he hadn't slept for days. He stared at me now with a dumbfounded expression.

"The key?" he repeated, and glanced past me toward David and Royce. Then he looked back, took my hand, and folded my fingers around the key ring. "I won't need this anymore," he said quietly. "Keep it."

"No, I—I can't," I protested.

He leaned his face close to mine. His dark eyes were mesmerizing. "Please," he said, "listen to me." His words were precise, commanding. "Get the Wild Goose. Morro Bay Mail Rentals."

"What?"

He squeezed my hand until his wide wedding band cut into my fingers. Then abruptly he released me and walked past me toward Royce. The two men spoke in harsh, whispered tones as they stalked together out of the hangar. I glanced again at the initialed key ring, shrugged, and slipped it into my canvas shoulder bag.

CHAPTER FOUR

When I joined David and Clarence at the counter, the two men were absorbed in conversation. "So there's absolutely no way for us to fly out today?" David was saying. "Not even if we drove to Santa Maria?"

"Nope. The fog's socked in all the way to San Luis Obispo," replied Clarence. "Looks like you and the little missus are stuck here, buddy."

"We're not married," I corrected.

"Well, yahoo!" said Clarence, winking at David and waving his hand with a flourish. His eyes rolled heavenward.

"This trip is strictly business," I said crisply. "I'm taking his secretary's place for the day."

"Well, you're a mighty purty substitute," Clarence said as his lecherous eyes swept over me.

David let out an exasperated sigh. "Well, Michelle, it looks like we're going to have to find a place to stay tonight."

"Oh, David, is that really necessary?"

"Yes. Clarence can't get my airplane parts until Monday."

Clarence cocked his blue, oil-stained visor cap and cut in with, "Ain't going to find no motel around here neither. There's a bloomin' flower growers' convention in town." He laughed raucously at his own feeble humor.

David bristled with impatience. "So you're saying we're stuck here in this airport?"

"Oh, David, no! I'm not sleeping in this freezing airport. I'll call my friend Jackie first."

"In Morro Bay? You can't ask her to come out in this fog." He scowled. "I'll rent a car and we'll find a vacancy somewhere near here."

"Same problem," Clarence shot back. "No cars available. Not in these boondocks."

"Surely we can call a taxi," I asserted.

"Aw, you don't have to do that," relented Clarence. "I'll rent you one of my beauties for a price. I got a special '59 Chevy Impala Coupe in the next hangar. You should see my collection of restored Chevys."

I touched David's arm. "First, I'd really like to telephone Jackie. If we're going to be stuck here this weekend, I'd love to see her."

David frowned. "You can call her, but let me call Eva first and see what she can accomplish from her end. I'll have to spend most of this weekend doing business over the phone."

Clarence shoved his black, grease-laden phone across the counter. "Here, use this. I'll add it to your bill."

"That won't be necessary," said David. "We'll use my credit card."

Minutes later, as David concluded his conversation with Eva, I removed my small writer's notebook from my canvas bag and found Jackie's number. David handed me the receiver, his expression quite businesslike. I dialed and listened to the hollow, distant ringing. There was a click, then a faint, hushed voice came over the wire. "Hello?"

"Jackie, is that you?" I asked.

"Who is this?"

"It's Michelle, your old college roommate."

There was a long pause. "Michelle . . . where are you?"

"You wouldn't believe where I am," I laughed. "Somewhere near Santa Maria."

"Are you coming to see me?"

"Oh, I can't. David—my boss—and I are stuck here in this miserable airport. We had plane trouble."

Jackie's voice emerged in a sob. "Oh, Michelle, you've got to come. I need you!"

"What's wrong?"

Jackie spoke with a brokenness that chilled me. "My husband—he was killed yesterday."

"Not Steve!"

"It was terrible, Michelle. His car plunged into a ravine."

"We're coming, Jackie," I said impulsively. "We'll be there as soon as we can."

I hung up the receiver and searched David's eyes.

He gazed back with disapproval. "Why did you tell her we're coming? I told you I have work to do."

Tears sprang to my eyes. "Jackie's husband was killed yesterday in a terrible accident."

"Killed?" echoed David. He took my hand. "I'm so sorry, Michelle. What happened?"

"His car went over a cliff."

"What's the man's name?" Clarence cut in brusquely.

"Steve Turman," I said. "He was my best friend's husband."

Clarence's eyes narrowed. "Then you knew the man?"

"No, I never met him."

He expelled a hefty sigh. "It seems to me I read about it in the paper this morning. Too bad," he said, shaking his head.

I looked again at David. "Please, I've got to go to Jackie. Will you drive me?"

"Michelle, this is no kind of weather for driving."

"I promised her I'd come. She can't be alone now."

"She must have friends nearby—"

"*I'm* her friend, David."

David's voice grew confidential. "Listen, Michelle. Eva's arranging a charter flight out of Santa Maria for us in the morning. You know how important this San Jose deal is for me. If we sign this contract, it'll open up opportunities throughout the San Francisco area."

"So that's the real reason you won't drive me to Jackie's. Not the weather!" I turned decisively to Clarence. "I'll rent your Chevy Coupe, Mr. Harvey, and drive myself." Then, glaring at David, I spewed, "I assume your competent Eva will be able to arrange a last-minute replacement for me in San Jose."

David's right eye muscle pulsated. "I trust you're not suggesting a *permanent* replacement?"

I wavered. David couldn't be serious. Was my job actually on the line? "I wasn't contemplating quitting, if that's what you mean, Mr. Ballard."

"Oh, we're back to *mister*, are we?"

"Well, aren't you pulling rank on me?"

"Be reasonable, Michelle."

I tossed my head defiantly. "I have no other but a woman's reason."

David broke into a spontaneous grin. "Shakespeare?"

"What of it?"

"*Taming of the Shrew?*"

"*Two Gentlemen of Verona.*"

David slipped a placating arm around my shoulder. "And all you want is *one* gentleman from Ballard Design?"

I was trembling, close to tears. "One would help."

"You win. I'll drive you." His fingertips pressed persuasively into my arm. "But in the morning, one way or another, I'm going on to San Jose. Alone, if necessary."

Looking relieved, Clarence broke in with, "I'll get the car for you." He charged around the counter and started out of the hangar in a lumbering run.

Minutes later, after tossing our overnight cases into the trunk of the Impala, David slipped into the front seat beside me. He smiled reassuringly. "We're on our way."

I sank against the cushioned backrest and stretched out my legs. Crippling exhaustion washed over me. In a whisper I said, "I still can't believe Steve Turman is dead."

"Death is always a shock," said David. The compassion in his voice stirred me.

"I'm sorry I was so short-tempered a few minutes ago. It's just that when I heard the news about Steve . . ."

"No problem." Then, changing the subject, David said, "I was surprised you told Clarence you had never met Steve."

"I never did. But I felt like I knew him from Jackie's letters."

"What kind of work did he do?"

"He was an insurance salesman and traveled a lot. Jackie met him while flying home for semester break. It was a whirlwind romance. She left school two months later to marry him. Stevie Jr. was born within the year. Jackie never finished her sophomore classes."

"It's going to be hard on the little guy, losing his father."

"But it'll be harder on Jackie. She was always the dependent type. Her family was wealthy and she was a social butterfly. She could have had any guy at Hopewell she wanted. But when she met Steve, that was it. No one else would do."

David bent forward, peering through the windshield. The wipers swished rhythmically, squeaking across the pane, permitting fractional glimpses of the road ahead. The fog was rolling over us, wave upon wave. "I'm not sure how far we're going to get," he said.

I shivered involuntarily. "How long will the drive take?"

"In this weather? Two hours at least."

"I'm freezing!"

"I tried the heat," said David, "but when Clarence

restored this old beauty to mint condition, he forgot to connect the heater." He patted the space beside him. "Scoot over close to me. I'll keep you warm." With a chuckle, he added, "Don't worry, I'm perfectly harmless."

My tone was cynical. "I've never met a harmless man yet."

"So what was his name?"

"Whose name?" I said evasively, thinking immediately of Scott.

"The guy who gave you such a skeptical attitude toward men."

"From what I've heard around the office, David, you're not exactly ready to accommodate a woman in your life either."

"Hey, that's a low blow."

"I didn't mean to be so blunt. I'm just a bit touchy on the subject myself."

"That's okay. You're right about me. But what happened was a long time ago."

"For me, his name was Scott," I admitted, my voice breaking slightly.

"The boyfriend who visited you at Hopewell?"

I nodded. "Actually, he was my fiance." I paused. "And who was it for you, David?"

He gave me a half-glance. "Her name was Cheryl. She was very young and beautiful, and I was in love."

"But something happened?"

"The war. Two tours in Vietnam. Cheryl and I were going to be married on my first R and R in Hawaii." His shadowed jaw twitched slightly. "But when I met her plane in Honolulu, she wasn't on it."

"Why not?"

There was an unexpected vulnerability in David's

expression. "Would you believe it? When I telephoned her home, her mother said she was on her honeymoon—with someone else."

"Oh, David." I reached out and touched his arm.

"But something positive did come from it all. The emptiness drove me to seek some meaning in my life. A fellow Navy pilot used to talk to me about God. I always avoided him and called him 'preacher boy.' But when I got back from R and R after losing Cheryl, I was ready to listen. My friend got me started in the Navigator's Bible study course. One night a few weeks later, I stood on the deck of our aircraft carrier, feeling desperately alone. As the waves lashed against the ship, I cried out in the darkness, 'Oh, God—if there is a God—take over this wretched life of mine.' " David's voice was deep, tremulous. "There was no clap of thunder, no great flash in the sky, but I was suddenly at peace. I knew God was real."

"So Christianity turned out to be the answer for you?"

"Yes, Michelle. God became real to me in the Person of His Son, Jesus Christ." David smiled invitingly. "How about you? You attended Hopewell."

I gazed out the window. The foggy mist swirled eerily. "Your broken romance did more for you than mine did for me."

"What do you mean?"

"I usually don't talk much about it." I sighed, then said with a rush of words, "I grew up on the front pew of a Baptist church where my father was the head deacon. My parents are beautiful, loving people, but when I wanted to marry Scott, they opposed me. My pastor refused to perform the ceremony because Scott wasn't a Christian. I was convinced I could get Scott to accept Christ some-day, so we made plans to be married in the church across town. The wedding invitations were in the mail. Then, out of the blue, two weeks before the wedding, my fiance ran off with one of my closest friends. My pastor and my parents told me it was God's will. But what did they know? I was angry and humiliated. I felt like Christianity had failed me."

"So you think God let you down?"

"It sounds selfish, I suppose, but that's how I feel."

There were several moments of silence between us. Then David reached over and squeezed my hand. "I'll tell you one thing," he said, his voice soft, "whoever he was, he missed out on one very special gal."

I smiled my appreciation. "You know, it's funny."

"What is?"

"The way you puzzle me. One minute you seem so unapproachable and the next you're so—so human."

"Unapproachable? Is that why you always looked away whenever I saw you at the office?"

"I didn't want you to think I was one of those silly girls with a crush on her boss."

"My secretary Eva does her best to protect me from such scheming females. However, you've always had Eva's stamp of approval. And now, I might add, you have mine."

I felt my cheeks flush. "I never thought you even noticed me. At the office you always seemed so formal, so reserved, so aloof—you know, being the owner of the company and all."

"That bad, huh?" He laughed. "And here all the time I was hoping to get your attention."

"Really? I felt rather intimidated by you. Whenever I entered your plush office and saw you sitting behind that massive oak desk surrounded by those towering shelves of books, I felt as if I were approaching deity."

He eyed me with a mischievous twinkle. "I've been called a lot of things in my time, but that's a first."

"But that was before today," I added quickly.

"Oh, you mean now I'm different?"

"I don't know how to explain it. We've shared so much together these past few hours. When we were in the airplane . . . it's just that when you think you're going to die with someone, it changes things. You feel as if you have this thing between you—a common bond."

He nodded. "I know what you mean. You're much more to me now than just that attractive lady behind the typewriter in the central office."

For the next half hour, as we rode in companionable silence, I felt myself growing drowsy, hypnotized by the steady drone of the engine. My head lolled against David's shoulder.

The next thing I knew, David was calling me from a great distance. "Wake up, Michelle, we're here." I roused from sleep, sat up, and stretched. My muscles were stiff; my neck ached. I fluffed my hair and straightened my blazer. "We're at Jackie's already?"

"This is Atascadero Road and it says Turman on the mailbox."

Before us stood a sprawling two-story farmhouse set back some distance from the narrow asphalt road. The house was surrounded by towering eucalyptus trees, a ghostly gothic apparition in the ethereal mist. There was a muted yellow glow from the eaves of the rambling front porch.

David drove slowly up the driveway and parked in front of the house. He slipped out of the car and helped me out, and we climbed the expansive steps. David rang the bell. The chimes sang in response. A moment later the door opened. Jackie stood there, slender in a silk Oriental robe, framed by the living room light. Even without makeup she was stunning; her blond hair was pulled back carelessly from her small oval face; her green eyes shone through swollen lids.

"Jackie!"

We embraced wordlessly, and wept.

CHAPTER FIVE

At last Jackie's sobs subsided. I held her a moment longer, noting with alarm the frail shoulders and thin back—once fashionably thin, but now—

"I'm sorry, Michelle," Jackie began, drawing back and touching her wet cheeks with her graceful, tapered fingers. "Come in, please." She stepped aside with a sweeping, automatic gesture.

In the entryway my heels clicked over the polished oak floor, then sank into plush beige carpeting. Muted lighting gave a quiet dignity to the spacious brown-and-tan living room with its natural stone fireplace and open-beamed ceiling.

I introduced David. Jackie offered a distracted nod, then turned away, hugging her arms against her scant chest. The audacious twinkle of years ago, and her lofty bearing, were gone. Only the determined chin remained of the Jacquelyn Howard I remembered. Now she reminded me of a lost, ravaged child fending off the dark. I had never seen Jackie so painfully vulnerable.

"Let me take your coats," she said, her voice as tenuous as her frame. "The drive here must have been terrible. This weather—the fog. Sit down by the fire—I'll warm the coffee."

"No," I said. "*You* sit down. I'll get the coffee."

Jackie sank into a corner of the long, russet sofa with obvious relief, curling her legs under her. "Make yourself at home, Michelle."

"Don't worry. I always feel at home with you, Jackie." I found the generous, L-shaped kitchen, but when I inspected the refrigerator, I could think only of Old Mother Hubbard—it was nearly bare. Jackie had never rhapsodized over luscious pastries or culinary delicacies like I had, but this was ridiculous. It appeared she was on a permanent fast.

I returned to the living room. "When did you eat last, Jackie?"

She looked puzzled, as if the idea of food were foreign to her.

"Have you eaten today?" I persisted.

"No. Toast maybe. I don't remember. And coffee."

"How about an omelet?"

"No, you go ahead. You and David must be starved."

David and I exchanged concerned glances. Jackie obviously needed someone to watch out for her. I summoned my most enthusiastic voice and said,

"Remember the mean omelet I used to fix in college?"

"I thought it was *popcorn*," inserted David.

"That was the laundry room," I whispered back. I looked at Jackie. "We weren't supposed to cook anything in our dorm rooms, remember?"

"That didn't stop us," she noted.

"We had this little hot plate, David," I continued. "I made the best omelets in the world, with cheddar cheese and fresh mushrooms—"

"and green onions," Jackie added.

"If I can scrounge up enough stuff in the fridge, I'll fix one now—if you'll eat it, Jackie."

"I'll try—if you omit the onions."

Minutes later the three of us sat around Jackie's quaint soapstone wood stove in the dining room, devouring my fluffy, golden omelet. That is, David and I devoured; Jackie picked. No wonder she was skin and bones. She was wheezing, her breath coming in snatches—the first sign of her old asthma attacks. She had also developed a nervous gesture with her fingers. Jackie pulled at ravels, twisted her sash, and picked at invisible particles of lint. I had the irresistible urge to clamp her hands down firmly to keep them from moving. I wanted to reach through her nervous energy and distracted gaze to find the Jackie I loved and remembered.

"Please try to eat," I coaxed.

"I can't. I can't imagine ever being hungry again." She looked imploringly at me. "How could it have happened, Michelle? How can Steve be dead? He was supposed to be in Oakland. The police said he went over a cliff just miles from here, but he told me he was seeing a client in Oakland. They said he was heading out of town when it happened, but that doesn't make any sense. If he was so close, he would have been coming home."

"I don't know, Jackie," I sighed.

"Maybe the police will have some answers," David offered.

"I can't make myself believe he's gone," Jackie continued urgently, looking neither at David nor me. "I would feel it, wouldn't I? I'd feel his being dead. I'd know it in every part of me. But I don't feel anything. I'm numb. I expect him to walk in the door right this minute. I hear him calling me. His voice is in my head. I'm filled with the sound of him, his words. I feel his touch, smell his cologne in every room. He can't be gone, Michelle. He can't be!"

Jackie began to sob. I stooped down beside her chair and held her. "You don't have to talk about it if you don't want to, Jackie," I soothed.

She drew back and looked at me with an odd amazement on her face. "I've got to , Michelle. Don't you see? I want to talk. I've got to keep going over these things in my mind until they make sense. Somehow, God help me, I've got to make them real."

"You can't do it all tonight. You need to rest. You have yourself and your little boy to think of."

"I can't sleep."

"Have you called your doctor? Maybe he could prescribe something."

Jackie grimaced. "He can't help. I've been on sleeping pills for months now." Shame crept into her voice. "Steve is—I mean *was*—gone so often, for days at a time, on the road, you know? He had clients all over Northern California. I hated staying alone at night. I had a hard time sleeping, so the doctor gave me a prescription. But the pills don't help anymore.

Nothing helps. How can anything ever help me again...without Steve?"

"Have you called your parents in Florida?"

Jackie bristled. "What do you think? They disowned me when I married Steve. Why should I call them now and hear them gloat?"

"Oh, Jackie, they'd never do that. They still love you."

"Have you contacted Steve's family?" David interjected.

"Steve was a foster child. He had no family...except for us."

"I'm sorry." David's voice was gentle. "Perhaps there are other details we can help with? Funeral arrangements?"

Jackie looked momentarily as if her face might shatter. "I—I haven't even seen Steve since the accident. The coroner says I can't see the—the body. He says my Steve is—he says he's—mutilated—"

"But I thought the coroner always had someone identify the body—" I began.

"How?" Jackie's voice peaked. "When Steve's car plunged over the ravine, it burst into flames. My darling was burned beyond recognition!"

David reached over and touched Jackie's hand. "Would you like me to call a mortuary for you?"

"The coroner's office helped me select one. They'll be transferring Steve's body to Ocean View Mortuary later this evening. In the morning I'll go see him. I'll insist they let me see him."

"Have you talked with your minister about a service?" David inquired.

Jackie glanced sheepishly at me. "I don't have a church. I haven't attended since college. Steve never entered a church—ever," she added mournfully.

"You'll need someone," I ventured.

"I never had your faith, Michelle. In college you were always ready to pray or go to church, but I always said I didn't need anybody."

"I meant you'll need someone to conduct the services," I corrected awkwardly. I realized I should say something about God's willingness to comfort, but the words stuck in my throat. I looked expectantly at David, thinking, *You could conduct the service. You'd know what to say.*

"The mortuary should provide a chapel and someone to officiate," David offered.

"I just want a simple graveside service. Steve and I had few mutual friends. I mean, people were coming and going around here all the time, but they were Steve's friends, not mine. I wouldn't even know how to contact them now. And I'm not sure I'd want to anyway."

"What about your neighbors?" I asked.

"We're a mile from anyone. Steve always said he didn't want nosy neighbors poking around."

"It must be terribly lonely for you," I noted. "You always loved being surrounded by people."

"Stevie Jr. keeps me company." Jackie smiled wanly, then reached over and touched her wood stove with her fingertips. "And these last few months I've been busy remodeling our farmhouse."

"You've done a fantastic job, Jackie." Addressing David, I explained, "Jackie studied interior decorating in college. We had the most gorgeous dorm room on campus. But, of course, it was nothing like the splendor here. This place must have cost a fortune!"

Jackie nodded. "Steve's sales had increased tremendously this past year, so there was money enough to do whatever I pleased."

"Steve must have been a very generous husband."

"He wasn't always that way," replied Jackie. "When we were first married, money was tight. I was used to having so much that I really couldn't cope with poverty. We argued all the time. I guess I pushed Steve too much. But when we found this farmhouse, it was Steve's dream to renovate it."

I looked around approvingly. "After living in a string of foster homes as a child, he must have enjoyed having such a luxurious place of his own."

Jackie nodded. "I think Steve secretly wanted to prove he could give me a better home than anything my parents provided."

"He succeeded," I said softly.

Jackie tried a smile. "You'll see everything in the morning. The exterior is still gingerbread Gothic, but our architect gutted the interior and changed several small rooms into two large living areas. He added a new wing to the northeast corner. Steve kept a running account of all the improvements—Polaroid snapshots and all. Would you like to see them?" She brightened, momentarily animated as she talked of Steve's dream.

David was sleepy. I nudged him and answered for both of us. "We'd love to see the pictures, Jackie."

We followed Jackie back into the living room and settled beside her on the velvet sofa. David rested his elbow on its tucked roll arm, fighting sleep. He stretched out his lanky legs under the glass cocktail table. Jackie was too absorbed in the snapshots to notice David's stifled yawns. She seemed satisfied with his occasional, "Nice... good photography," as she handed him the photos.

Finally I asked, "Jackie, do you have any pictures of Steve?"

She reached for her wedding album beside the brass candelabra lamp on the end table and drew in a tremulous breath before opening the cover. The first picture showed Steve's broad hand resting on Jackie's, a shiny wide wedding band on his ring finger.

There was another of the wedding couple standing before a justice of the peace, with Jackie in a stylish, white, street-length dress. The next revealed the profile of a sandy-haired, handsomely groomed man smiling down at his bride.

"Oh, Michelle, I loved him so much," Jackie sighed. Her hands trembled now and her mouth went rigid as she turned to several lovely pastel pictures of the two of them embracing, signing the marriage certificate, and sharing cake and champagne. It struck me that Steve's death had irrevocably splintered the love and laughter of that wedding day. Suddenly I bitterly regretted asking to see pictures of Steve.

I was about to suggest we put the book away until I caught a glimpse of the last two photographs. Something in them curiously jogged my memory. It was a bewildering sensation—the feeling of seeing someone I should have known, perhaps did know—but from some time and place that had nothing to do with Jackie.

The photos were close-up shots of Steve and Jackie—one as they climbed into a sleek red automobile, and the other as they embraced in the back seat, their heads together, smiling conspiratorially into the camera. There was something in Steve's slender, handsome features and shrewd eyes that mesmerized me.

"Steve looks so familiar," I said aloud. "It's as if

we've met some—" Before I could finish the sentence, we heard a child scream.

Jackie leaped to her feet. "It's Stevie Jr.," she said in alarm. She rushed from the room and was back moments later with a sleepy toddler in her arms. Stevie Jr. was a blond, talcum-fragrant ball of fluff in flannels. He had round, red cheeks, a turned-up nose, and a full, pouting mouth. He clung to Jackie, squinting against the lights, rubbing his eye with his fist.

"He had a nightmare," Jackie explained.

The child whimpered, "Where's my daddy?"

Jackie rocked him in her arms. "It's okay, Honey. You just had a bad dream."

"Where's my daddy?" he persisted.

Jackie's expression crumbled. "Daddy had to go away," she whispered.

He shook his head. "I want Daddy!"

"I know, Darling," Jackie soothed. "Before Daddy left, he said, 'Tell Stevie I love him—' " She couldn't finish. She buried her face in Stevie's blond curls and wept.

CHAPTER SIX

It was nearly midnight before I finally crawled into bed in the small room on the northeast corner of the house. Outside there was still heavy fog and mist, its dampness penetrating through the windowpanes. I shivered as I snapped off the Tiffany lamp.

My body was exhausted, but rest eluded me. All I could think of was Steve Turman. Here I was a guest in the house of a man I never knew—would never know now—yet he permeated the room and my thoughts.

I kept thinking, *Dead at 29! What a tragedy! Had it been, as Jackie said, a mistake? Steve in the neighborhood when he was supposed to be hours away in Oakland? Had he been heading home unexpectedly, his plans changed? Did he know in those moments before crashing to the bottom of the ravine that he would die? Did he think of Jackie? of Stevie Jr.? of God?*

I shivered involuntarily and snuggled even deeper under the eiderdown quilt. Vague pictures of Steve from the wedding album converged and receded as I drifted in and out of a fitful sleep. Over and over it was the same dream, the same struggle between wakefulness and slumber.

I was dreaming heavily, caught in a strange agony, but I couldn't awaken myself. Steve was walking toward me from the end of a long tunnel, wearing his wedding boutonniere, his face surrealistic and distant. His footsteps echoed hollowly. I tossed. The obscure figure eluded me, fading out of my grasp.

I awakened suddenly. It was 3:00 A.M. Someone had called. I squinted into the darkness. "Who's there?" In my semiwakefulness I heard myself say again, "Mr. Mangano."

It was the same dream—Steve Turman coming toward me, serious, unsmiling. And I heard myself saying, shouting, "Mr. Mangano, I believe you dropped these keys. . . ."

The face was Paul Mangano's; no, Steve's. They blurred as one. I shook my head, desperate to clear my mind. Then I knew, felt it, feared it, grasped it. I sat bolt upright. I was certain that the sober, sandy-haired stranger at Meadowgreen Airport was Steve Turman, Jackie's husband.

Four sleepless hours later, just past 7:00 A.M., I made my way to the kitchen, pausing briefly by the curved, split-level stairway that led up to little

Stevie's room in the sleeping loft. I could hear Jackie already running Stevie's bathwater.

The kitchen was fragrant with freshly brewed coffee. I blinked against the sunlight spilling through the gingham-framed windows. David stood by the wide Spanish-tile counter, coffeepot in hand. "Want some?" he asked, smiling. His thick, dark hair was sleep-tangled. He was wearing burgundy slacks and a white polo shirt. Even in his bare feet he stood over six feet tall.

"You're up early," I said groggily, accepting the steaming mug he offered.

" A regular habit of mine. I like to catch the early stock report."

"How industrious."

"Pure greed." He grinned.

"I suppose you'll be taking off for San Jose this morning."

"And you'll be staying?"

I nodded. "Jackie needs me—at least until after the funeral."

David made no reply.

I set my coffee mug on the counter and tightened the sash on my powder-blue robe. "David, before you leave, I need to talk to you."

He eyed me curiously, arching his right brow. "It sounds serious."

I glanced back to make certain Jackie wasn't around.

"You looking for Jackie?"

"I don't want her to hear this."

"Isn't she still upstairs with Stevie?"

"I hope so."

David refilled our coffee cups and carried them over to the oak parquet dining table. We sat on cushioned, cane-back chairs, sipping our coffee. David was relaxed, unhurried, his head cocked my way, his gaze disconcerting. "What's on your mind?"

"Steve Turman."

"I suppose he's on all of our minds. His death was tragic."

"I don't mean his death. There's something else."

"Go on."

"Remember the wedding pictures Jackie showed us last night?"

"Vaguely. I'm not much for family albums."

"I know, and you were so tired. But do you remember me saying that Steve looked familiar?"

"So he reminds you of some long-lost cousin?"

"No. More like a stranger."

David's eyes met mine directly. "A stranger?"

"Yes. The man who bumped into me at the airport."

"Clarence Harvey?"

"No, not him! His customer. The sober, sandy-haired one."

"Mangano?" frowned David. "Paul Mangano?"

"He could be Steve Turman's twin brother."

"So? Everyone has a look-alike."

"I think it's more than that."

"What are you trying to say, Michelle?"

I shook my head, flustered. "In the middle of the night I was so sure. The idea woke me out of a sound sleep. I lay for hours thinking about it, replaying it in my mind."

"Replaying what? What are you talking about?"

Miserably I blurted it out. "I think Paul Mangano and Steve Turman are the same man!"

David threw back his head and laughed. "Just like

a writer," he exclaimed. "Seeking intrigue around every corner."

"But, David," I bristled, "they do look alike. It's uncanny."

"All right, for the sake of argument, how do you explain a dead man suddenly very much alive and catching a plane?"

"I can't explain it. But what if there's a mistake?"

"What if *you're* making the mistake, Michelle?"

"I can't help how I feel. There's something about that face—something in the eyes. I know it sounds crazy, but what if Steve was running out on Jackie, maybe leaving her for someone else?"

"Michelle, this isn't one of those dime-store mysteries. A man is dead. His widow is upstairs. How can you even suggest a cheap lovers' triangle?"

"I know how ridiculous it sounds. Don't you think I hate myself for even thinking it? But it's there—this nagging possibility—"

David reached across the table for my hand. "Michelle, I know it's hard for you to accept Steve's death. You'd rather consider any other alternative. But for Jackie's sake you've got to accept it. Steve Turman died two days ago in a terrible auto accident. He was already dead when we met Paul Mangano at the airport."

"I suppose you're right," I relented. "But I don't think I'll ever forget my dream last night."

"Let's hope for better dreams tonight," David said softly. His fingers pressed mine with a tenderness that made me flush. He was still holding my hand moments later when Jackie entered.

"Excuse me," she began tentatively. "I hope I'm not interrupting."

David released my hand slowly, without embarrassment. "No problem," he said. "We were just having coffee."

Even in the early morning hour I was aware of Jackie's casual elegance. She was stylish in her Vanderbilt jeans and mint georgette blouse with its stand-up collar and pleated bodice. Her long blond hair was smoothed back from her face and tied behind her neck with a matching green ribbon. Two delicately plaited French braids formed a halo in her hair.

I stole a quick glance at David, wondering if he was taken by her flawless complexion, high cheekbones, and small, regal nose. Her determined chin quivered slightly. "You're up early, Jackie," I said.

"Couldn't sleep. Besides," she said as we heard Stevie whooping down the stairs from the loft, "three-year-olds don't take to sleeping in."

Moments later, Stevie bounded into the kitchen in his corduroy pants and "Big Bird" shirt and came to an abrupt halt. "Daddy?" he squealed with excitement as he dashed toward David. As quickly, he stopped in his tracks, his large dark eyes flashing disappointment.

"That's David and Michelle, Stevie. Remember? You met them last night."

He scrambled back to his mother and buried his face against her legs. His small chest heaved frantically. From across the room we could hear the sudden wheezing. Jackie lifted Stevie up. "Daddy's gone," she said, her voice empty. Stevie nestled against her, rubbing one eye shyly. He was still breathing with difficulty.

"His asthma's been acting up lately," Jackie lamented. "As bad as mine." She moved mechanically to the kitchen counter, setting Stevie back down as she did so. "I'll get you some breakfast," she offered.

David pushed back his chair and stood. "I shine at flapjacks, if you'll point me to the Aunt Jemima's."

Jackie gestured gratefully toward the cupboard above the stove. "Up there. And there's orange juice in the freezer."

David looked at Stevie. "How about you helping me, Tiger?"

The boy nodded eagerly.

Jackie sat beside me and we watched with amusement as David cracked eggs into his batter and stirred vigorously. "What's your favorite animal, Stevie?" he questioned.

"My goose."

"I don't think I can make a goose," David said as he poured batter onto the hot griddle. "A dog maybe."

Stevie pointed to a stuffed yellow duck on the floor. "Make him," he said. "That's my goose."

"It looks like a duck to me." David poured more batter, then, moments later, tossed a goose-shaped flapjack in the air and caught it on the tip of his spatula. "Okay, Tiger, bring me your plate. Breakfast is on."

We were just finishing David's gourmet flapjacks when the wall phone jangled. I reached out automatically and answered, then cupped the mouthpiece and whispered to Jackie, "It's Ocean View Mortuary."

Jackie paled as I handed her the receiver. "Yes, this is Mrs. Turman," she said tentatively. "Yes, of course, you have my husband's body. What? His ring? What do you mean he's been transferred?" Jackie's voice grew shrill. "I don't know what you're talking about. I didn't authorize any transfer."

She began to tremble. Her words grew erratic. "No, no, of course I didn't transfer him because you offended me. I didn't transfer him at all! You don't have to be so indignant—no, I never heard of Seward Brothers Mortuary. I didn't sign any authorization!"

She turned to David in desperation and handed him the phone. "The funeral director insists I've released Steve's body to another mortuary. I don't know what's happening. You talk, please!"

David spoke for several moments, then hung up the phone and gazed soberly at us. "The man wants you to pick up Steve's wedding ring. He says he forgot to include it when they transferred Steve's body to Seward Brothers Mortuary."

"But why did they transfer him? It doesn't make any sense!"

"He says they had a signed authorization."

"But who gave them permission?" cried Jackie.

David flashed me a cryptic glance, then looked back at Jackie. "The man says it's your signature on the form."

Jackie's hysteria mounted. "But it's not—I didn't—I never even heard of Seward Brothers!"

CHAPTER SEVEN

While Jackie was upstairs composing herself, David telephoned Seward Brothers Mortuary, spoke in confidential tones for several moments, then hung up abruptly and turned to me. "That was a wasted phone call," he said with exasperation. "The girl was one of those bubble-headed receptionists who deliberately knows nothing. She said Mr. Seward, the funeral director, wouldn't be in until evening. I finally pressed her for an 8:00 P.M. appointment."

"She wouldn't tell you anything about why Steve's body was transferred there from Ocean View Mortuary?" I asked.

"Nothing. For every question I asked, she replied, 'You'll have to speak to Mr. Seward about that.' "

"You made the appointment for 8:00 P.M.?"

David nodded.

"But you're leaving for San Jose this morning."

"I was." He scowled. "I'd better call Eva and see how things stand with Blair Publishers. If I can't change my appointment, perhaps you could drive Jackie over to Seward Brothers this evening."

"Oh, David, I wish you were going to be here. Things are so complicated."

"Strange is more accurate," he returned. "I don't like the way that receptionist was so evasive with me. I had the feeling she was being coached by someone in the background."

"But why?"

"You tell me." He shrugged and reached for the telephone.

"While you're talking to Eva," I said, "I'll check on Jackie and see if she's ready to go pick up Steve's ring."

Fifteen minutes later I returned to the living room. David stood staring out the bay window, a troubled expression on his face.

"Jackie will be down in a minute," I began. I paused. "Is something the matter, David?"

His gaze remained fixed. "I've made arrangements to stay through the weekend, Michelle."

"That's wonderful, David. It's a relief to know you'll be here." When he didn't respond, I asked in alarm, "Did Blair Publishers cancel their deal?"

David looked over and offered a sardonic smile. "No, they haven't canceled. But in this computer business, until you've signed the contract, you're never sure of a sale."

"Then maybe you should go on to San Jose."

"Some things are more important than business."

"But not if you're going to lose out financially," I countered.

"I didn't have peace about leaving, Michelle."

"What does peace have to do with it?"

"I just felt God impressing me to stay. I don't understand it, but I've learned through hard experience to listen."

I turned away. I didn't know how to answer him. "I'll see what's holding Jackie," I said.

An hour later David was still pensive as he drove Jackie's Buick Regal through the open wrought-iron gates of Ocean View Mortuary in San Luis Obispo. Jackie sat in the backseat with Stevie Jr. nestled against her. She hadn't said a word the entire trip. As David pulled to a stop beside the Spanish-style stucco building, Stevie sat forward eagerly and exclaimed, "Are we going to see my daddy?"

There was profound silence. At last Jackie managed, "We're going to get Daddy's ring, darling."

"Can I have Daddy's ring, Mommy?"

"When you grow up, Honey."

"I all grown up," he insisted.

David opened Jackie's door and lifted Stevie out. "You are a big boy," he said, carrying him up the flowered walkway. Jackie and I followed, arm-in-arm. I could feel her beginning to tremble as we opened the massive carved oak doors.

We followed David across the expansive hallway to the receptionist's desk. A matronly woman with cropped hair and toneless gray eyes offered a professional smile. "May I help you?"

David introduced Jackie and said, "Mr. Benoit telephoned us about picking up Mr. Turman's ring."

The woman gestured toward a closed door. "He's with a family now. He'll be with you shortly."

David offered Jackie a straight-back chair, but she refused. Meanwhile, Stevie Jr. pulled away from David and wandered across the lobby to inspect a large floral arrangement. He squatted and sniffed at a yellow gladiola. Jackie was beside him immediately, yanking him away. "Your asthma, Stevie!" she scolded.

Stevie darted from her grasp and dashed straight into the shins of a staid little man we soon learned was Oscar Benoit. The balding, bespectacled man leaned down and placed his hand on the boy's shoulder. "Goodness, young man," he exclaimed with a nasal twang, "this old place hasn't seen such energy in many a day!" Then, glancing over the top of his glasses, he said, "My receptionist tells me you're the Turman family. Why don't we step inside my office?"

Even inside Mr. Benoit's office, Jackie refused to be seated. Watching her, I could sense the roiling tension she was barely able to suppress. The flutter of her hands in constant, futile gestures betrayed her agitation. "We're just here to pick up my husband's ring," she announced. "But I want you to know I had nothing to do with his body being transferred to another mortuary."

Mr. Benoit's beady eyes flashed behind thick lenses as he took a document from the neatly stacked papers on his desk. "Then how do you explain this, Mrs. Turman?"

I peered over Jackie's shoulder at the official paper she held with trembling fingers. "That's my signature," she uttered, "but it can't be. I never saw this form before."

"Well, Seward Brothers presented this very document when they took possession of Mr. Turman's body," related Mr. Benoit. "It was a highly unusual situation, removing a body from the premises when our arrangements had already been made, but I assume you had your own reasons for the transfer. I certainly observed no irregularities in the document."

"I tell you, I never saw that document!"

Mr. Benoit's eyes narrowed. "This is your signature, is it not?"

"Yes, but—I mean, I never signed it. I don't understand how any of this could have happened."

I could tell by the expression on Mr. Benoit's face that he didn't believe Jackie, that he obviously saw her only as a confused, distraught young widow. Without pressing the issue further, he quickly tore off the carbon copy of the authorization form and handed it to her. Then, in a mildly coddling voice, he said, "I'm sorry, Mrs. Turman, about this entire misunderstanding, but I trust you'll find Seward Brothers Mortuary quite satisfactory."

"But I didn't choose Seward Brothers," Jackie protested weakly.

Mr. Benoit turned on a placating smile as he picked up a small Manila envelope. "Here is your husband's ring, Mrs. Turman."

David supported Jackie's arm as we walked back through the cavernous vestibule, our heels clicking on the ceramic tile. Stevie Jr. lagged behind, running his open hands over the plush red velvet wallpaper. I nudged him along as unobtrusively as possible, out the door, and down the steep cement steps to Jackie's car.

A half-hour later, as David swung the automobile

onto Atascadero Road, I heard a small gasp from the backseat. I looked around at Jackie. She was staring transfixed at a narrow gold band in the palm of her hand. "This isn't Steve's ring," she said in disbelief.

"What do you mean?" I asked.

"This ring—it's someone else's, not Steve's."

"Are you sure?"

"Of course I'm sure!" She examined it scornfully. "Steve's band was wide. And look, even the inscription is wrong." She was crying now. "This ring has the initials 'P.M.' My husband's ring says, 'Jackie loves Steve.' "

CHAPTER EIGHT

For lunch that afternoon I fixed steaming bowls of tomato soup and toasted cheese sandwiches. Stevie Jr. fell asleep at the table, so David carried him up to his youth bed in the loft. Jackie, leaving her food untouched, excused herself, saying, "I have a pounding migraine."

"So much for my culinary skills," I remarked privately to David when he returned from the loft.

He tweaked my cheek and said, "I asked Jackie about borrowing her Buick this afternoon. We need to return Clarence Harvey's Impala to Meadowgreen

Airport—if you don't mind driving one of the cars there."

"I'll take that gorgeous Buick," I teased. "But is it necessary to go today? We may have trouble making it back in time for Jackie's 8:00 P.M. appointment with Seward Brothers Mortuary."

"We'll make it."

"But Mr. Harvey said there was no rush in returning the car."

"It's not the car, Michelle."

I frowned. "You mean we borrowed something else?"

"Not from Clarence Harvey. But I'm about to borrow something from Jackie—besides her Buick."

My curiosity was sparked by the intensity in David's voice. "Are we going back because you're worried about the repairs on your plane?" I persisted.

"No, but the plane will be my excuse," he replied as he strode to the living room. I followed and watched puzzled as he removed a photo from Jackie's wedding album.

"What are you doing?"

He leaned his face close to mine and spoke confidentially. "While I'm checking on the plane, I'll also be checking out your earlier suspicions regarding Mr. Paul Mangano."

"You mean the resemblance between Mr. Mangano and Steve?" I asked incredulously.

"You got it."

"But you scoffed at my—my dime-store mystery."

"There are too many strange things going on here, Michelle—Steve's accident so close to home when he was supposed to be in Oakland, the transfer of his body without Jackie's knowledge—"

"Then you believe Jackie didn't sign that authorization?"

"I'm beginning to."

"What else?"

"The wrong ring."

"So what?"

"I would have considered it a simple mixup, except for the initials, P.M."

"P.M.?" I mulled it over. "Oh, David, you don't mean—you don't think—Paul Mangano?"

"It's possible. I intend to find out for sure."

"How?" I asked.

"By seeing if Clarence Harvey notices a resemblance between Steve and Paul Mangano."

"What if he does?"

"Then maybe he can help us locate Mr. Mangano."

"And if Mr. Mangano turns out to be Steve, what then?"

David frowned. "Then we've been making funeral arrangements for the wrong man."

"Oh, David, I never thought of that. Who could it be?"

"Let's face that question later."

"But it would mean Steve had run out on Jackie—maybe for another woman."

"We don't know that, Michelle."

"What other reason would there be?"

"I don't know. Financial losses maybe? A fake insurance claim? Something serious enough for him to want his wife to think he's dead."

"Oh, David—!"

"For Jackie's sake, I almost hope our suspicions are wrong."

"One way or another, David, we've got to find the truth."

"Then let's get going." David handed me the keys to the Buick and said, "Drive carefully."

"I will. Just don't lose me."

He chuckled. "Why would I want to lose you? I just found you." Unexpectedly he leaned down and brushed a kiss on the top of my head.

I thought about that kiss all the way to Meadow-green Airport.

The plain, galvanized buildings glittered in the sunlight, almost blinding me as I pulled up beside Harvey's Hangar Cafe. David was leaning against the Impala, waiting for me. "We're in luck," he said. "Paul Mangano's pilot is apparently employed by Meadowgreen Airport. He's having lunch inside."

"Did he recognize you?"

"I just saw him through the window."

"Well, what are we waiting for?"

We went inside and casually sat at the counter beside the blond pilot. "Hello, we're back again," David told the gum-chewing waitress. "How about a bowl of your terrific homemade vegetable soup."

"Coming right up." The brassy, bubble-haired woman gazed curiously at me.

"The same," I said, "and a Coke."

"Coffee here," said David. He cast a sidelong glance at the pilot who sat reading a newspaper. "Pardon me, aren't you the pilot who was here yesterday when my Bonanza was grounded?"

The sullen-faced man looked over, his small brown eyes appraising David coolly. "Maybe."

"You were trying to fly out a passenger by the name of Paul Mangano."

The man rolled his newspaper and slapped it on the counter. "What's it to you, mister?"

David chuckled uneasily. "I'm sorry. I'm not getting off to a very good start here. Let me introduce myself. I'm David Ballard and this is Michelle Merrill."

I peered around David and offered a tentative smile. "Hi," I said.

The man glared back, his left eye squinting involuntarily. He was almost handsome, except for a surly arrogance in the curl of his lips.

Our buxom waitress returned with our soup and drinks. "Come on, Royce," she chided, "tell them your name like a good boy." She looked at us and winked, "Royce ain't much for talking. But he has other talents."

The pilot reached out for her wrist and snapped back, "I'll do my own talking, baby."

She freed her hand and leaned cozily across the counter toward Royce, her plum-colored lips nearly touching his wispy blond hair. "You can hold my hand anytime you want, Honey, but don't break my wrist. Save that for your other ladies."

"Can it, Sylvia!"

She whirled back to David and me. "His name's Royce Adams, mister. But I don't know why anyone would want to know."

"I'm sorry, Mr. Adams," David said. "We didn't mean to offend you. We just thought perhaps you could help us."

"How?" he grunted.

David handed him the picture of Steve Turman. "Do you recognize this man?"

Royce stared down at the photo, his facial muscle twitching nervously. "Of course not. Why should I?"

"We thought this might be your passenger, Mr. Mangano."

"Not a chance."

"Would you mind telling us where you flew Mr. Mangano?" persisted David.

Royce's dark eyes narrowed to menacing slats. "Nowhere. We were socked in with fog. Remember?"

"Well, then, what was Mr. Mangano's destination?"

"How would I know?"

"I was under the impression Mr. Mangano was your friend."

"Hardly."

"Then you have no idea where he went from here?"

Royce reached for a cigarette from his shirt pocket and muttered, "No idea whatever."

I could tell David was growing heated, so I touched his arm and said, "Never mind, David. It's obvious Mr. Adams can't help us."

David snatched the photo from Royce, threw several bills on the counter and stood abruptly. "Come on, Michelle. Let's go check on my Bonanza." He hurried me outside before I could even offer a feeble goodbye.

As we made our way past the hangar toward the airstrip, we spotted Clarence Harvey beside David's plane. His squatty figure was bent over a workbox; his red grease cloth, stuffed in his hip pocket, was bright as a flag.

"Hi, Mr. Harvey," I called cheerily. "We brought your Impala back safely."

He straightened and waved a beefy arm. "Howdy, folks! Hope you ain't counting on this plane today. But don't worry. I ordered the parts and we'll have this beauty ready early next week."

"I wish it could be sooner, Clarence," said David as we approached the Bonanza. "But I do appreciate all your efforts."

"I thought you had a business meeting in San Jose," the rotund man remarked. "So what are you doing here?"

"You know how it goes—the best-laid plans of mice and men..."

"Say no more," he chuckled. "So what can I do for you today?"

"Just answer a question or two."

"Sounds simple enough. Try me, especially if it relates to planes."

"Not planes," David answered, "but passengers. We're looking for someone who was here yesterday."

"We didn't have many passengers, not in that pea soup."

"What about Paul Mangano?"

Clarence's eyes flashed with curiosity. "What about him?"

"We're hoping we can locate him—for a friend of ours."

"Not likely."

"No way to get in touch with him?" David persisted.

Clarence yanked the grease rag from his pocket and mopped his brow. "I don't expect ever to see that fella again in my life. He was downright cranky when we wouldn't fly him out of here."

"Didn't he say where he was going when he left?"

Clarence shrugged. "To the nearest airport, I suppose. He was determined to leave, one way or another."

I slipped my hand in David's arm. "Why don't we show Mr. Harvey the picture?" I urged.

David's cheek muscle tightened; the scar in the cleft of his chin protruded slightly. He took the photo from his pocket and handed it to Clarence. "We're wondering if you recognize this man?"

Clarence was silent a moment, then boomed, "I don't know the fella, but I wouldn't mind knowing the pretty bride by his side."

"That's my friend, Jackie Turman," I explained.

One of Clarence's craggy brows lifted. "Who?"

"My friend in Morro Bay."

"You don't mean that poor young thing who lost her husband?"

"The same," David replied. "But, Mr. Harvey, do you think the man could be Paul Mangano?"

Clarence studied the photograph intently. "From what little I remember of Mr. Mangano, he could look a mite bit like him. This man's younger though, better looking."

"Then you don't think it's Mr. Mangano?"

"Hardly." Clarence handed the picture back to David. "Why the sudden interest in this Mangano fellow?"

"Like I said," David answered, "I was trying to help a friend. We thought if we could find Mangano..."

"Not here." Clarence gave us a crooked smile. "Crazy," he said with a perplexed shake of the head. "Passengers come and go. We just log in their destinations. In this case, the man never flew out of Meadowgreen Airport."

"Then you don't recall his destination?"

"East, somewhere."

"Thanks." David tucked the photo back in his

pocket. Then, taking my hand, he emitted a defeated sigh. "Sorry we bothered you, Mr. Harvey."

"No bother." Clarence wiped his hands with the grease rag and turned back to his workbench.

As we walked away, he called after us, "Royce Adams might be the one to check with. He's the last one who saw Mangano."

"Thanks," David said again. "We've already checked with Adams."

CHAPTER NINE

David took the wheel of the Buick and we started the drive back to Jackie's place. For 20 minutes we rode in silence, David's face masking the agitation he was obviously feeling inside. The only sound was the whir of traffic as it sped past us. To our left the Pacific Ocean lapped at the coastline, the waves breaking in fury against jutted rocks.

Finally, when I could stand it no longer, I mumbled an apology. "I'm sorry, David. I didn't mean to make us look like such fools. If it hadn't been for my silly dream that Steve Turman was...that Paul Mangano was..." I shrugged helplessly.

David gave me a passive glance; then a half-amused smile played on his lips. "No need to apologize. We simply did what we had to do."

"But Clarence Harvey thinks we're crazy."

"Does he?" David reflected. "And if he does, does it matter?"

"It matters that I got you into a ridiculous situation." I swallowed—my pride, partly. "And it matters if I made you angry."

"My silence wasn't anger, Michelle." He squeezed my hand to reassure me. "We're onto something. I was just trying to put the pieces together."

"I thought all the pieces crumbled back there at Meadowgreen."

His hand stayed warm against mine. "As my secretary Eva would say, something's wrong in Denmark. I can't put my finger on it. And you're right—Clarence does think we're a bit crazy, and with good reason. We took off like a couple of amateur sleuths without thinking things through." His eyes stayed on the road, but the tension lines around his mouth relaxed. In a way, he wasn't even talking to me; he was talking out loud, working out the details for himself, for us both.

I waited with growing impatience.

"There's a problem," he went on. "But it's back at the farmhouse or at the mortuary. We'll start there. As it stands, we have nothing to go on except your dream and my premonition. Local authorities would frown on both. But I do have a definite feeling that there's more to Steve Turman's death than a charred body."

I trembled. "What will we tell Jackie?"

"Nothing. Until we have something more definite." He took a quick glance from the freeway to his wristwatch. "We have ample time to be at Seward Brothers for our 8:00 P.M. appointment. Somewhere along the line, the pieces will fit together."

My stomach knotted uncomfortably. "If only we really knew who died in that accident."

David's eyes were somber. "Until we know for certain, we'll go right on burying Steve."

"That's awful."

"Do you have a better idea?"

"No."

"Then trust me, Michelle."

I wanted to say, *Why should I trust any man?*

It was as if David guessed my thoughts, for he quickly added, "This morning—and yesterday morning—I asked the Lord for direction. Yesterday it was with the belief that a contract with Blair Publishers was at my fingertips, a crucial business deal almost consummated." He grinned. "I didn't ask for Eva to be sick. I didn't ask for plane trouble. As far as I was concerned I was God's for the whole 24 hours."

"And my rushing you off to Jackie's may have ruined that business deal!"

"Hush, Michelle," he soothed. "Neither of us planned the detours in this trip. I've always felt my business is God's business. I don't understand what God has for us in this odyssey, but I'm confident He has our best interest at heart."

"Even if it costs you the Blair contract?"

"Michelle, you know what I'm talking about. Seeking God's direction and blessing is not new to you. My Vietnam conversion wasn't just a get-me-out-of-here promise. God's leadership is important to me on a daily basis. From what you've told me, it once was to you too."

I pulled my hand free, resentment brewing. David made no attempt to stop me.

Instead, he gave me a caring smile. "I wish we could be partners in prayer during this bewildering situation, not just self-appointed detectives."

I didn't reply. I was too busy fighting back tears.

The miles sped by. I kept thinking of David's words: *God has our best interest at heart.* I knew David was right. It went along with my training as a child. My own godly parents lived out that theme in their lives. Hopewell College had attempted to instill that same truth in me. But never before had anyone couched the words so simply as David had done.

"You're right," I said finally.

"I am?" He seemed surprised. "About what?"

I shrugged. I didn't trust myself to admit my need, to tell David that my spiritual life was more sham than reality. But then, didn't he already know that? I gazed out the window at the blue foaming Pacific as wave upon wave crashed futilely against the unyielding rocks. Inside I knew I was still running.

That evening I was still in a subdued frame of mind as we sat in the vestibule of Seward Brothers Mortuary. The room matched my mood with its heavy velvet drapes, fruitwood tables, and softly glowing ginger-jar lamps.

While we waited to be ushered into the office for our scheduled appointment, I linked arms with Jackie to offer my unspoken support. Only the door chimes playing "Nearer My God to Thee" broke the hushed atmosphere. I balked instinctively at the sickening sweet smell of lilies and carnations that permeated the room.

"Thank goodness, Stevie's at the sitter's," Jackie wheezed. "These flowers would wreak havoc with his asthma."

"It's after eight," David complained as he paced the floor near the mahogany reception desk. He glanced impatiently down the long hallway toward the chapel.

Finally, at 8:15, a massive carved door opened and a swarthy gentleman stepped out. He was fortyish, with an olive complexion and slick black hair that might have been a toupee. Bushy brows shrouded his deep-set eyes.

"Good evening, I'm Leon Seward." His voice was soft-spoken, his demeanor composed. "Perhaps we could talk more privately inside," he said, gesturing toward the office behind him.

As we took our seats in the compact room, Mr. Seward introduced us to his older brother Zachary. Except for Zachary's mustache, the two men possessed an uncanny resemblance.

Zachary Seward sat unsmiling behind the desk, his manner cool and reserved. A fringe of silver streaked his wavy hair. His face was narrower than Leon's, but his dominant nose and pursed lips were identical to his brother's.

Zachary leaned forward, his elbows resting on the desk top. Even as he greeted us he twisted a silver pen in his left hand. "There are a number of decisions for you to make, Mrs. Turman," he said matter-of-factly, his Adam's apple bobbing with each word. "The casket—we have a large selection to choose from—stainless steel, copper, wood—"

"I never sent my husband here," Jackie declared.

"If finances are a problem, Mrs. Turman, we have a simple pine casket," Zachary continued, smoothing the corner of his mustache. "But I'm sure you'll want something more fitting, more elaborate, in a solid cherry or maple."

"I want to see my husband," Jackie said shrilly.

Zachary and Leon exchanged knowing glances. Leon spoke first. "I'm sorry, Mrs. Turman. That won't be possible."

"Why not?"

"You did understand the nature of your husband's injuries?" Leon inquired.

Jackie gripped the arms of her chair; her knuckles blanched. "I'm well aware of how my husband died. And I want to see his body now."

David spoke up. "I believe Mrs. Turman has the right to see her husband. We'll be with her," he said, including me in his gaze.

Zachary Seward slapped his pen on the desk. "Absolutely not." He turned his indignation against David. "Mr. Ballard, have you no mercy for this grief-stricken widow? If she views the body, I will not be responsible for the tragic consequences."

Jackie searched David's face. "Please, David. Please, help me."

David tried again. "Perhaps I could view the body for her?"

Zachary remained adamant in his refusal. "Don't press me to do something we'd all regret." He chose his words carefully. "Mr. Turman's body, particularly his face, was burned beyond recognition."

Jackie was crying uncontrollably, near collapse. I gathered her against me. "David, we've got to take Jackie home."

David glared at the Seward brothers. "We'll leave now. But we'll be back. The subject is far from closed."

"Check with the coroner," Zachary said smoothly. "He will confirm the injuries. We are not trying to be unfair." He was precise as he addressed David. "We want to do what is best for Mrs. Turman."

At the door, he added, "We will have to make arrangements for the service soon, tomorrow at the latest."

An hour later, after picking up Stevie Jr. from the sitter's, we pulled into the Turman driveway. The house was shadowed in eerie darkness.

"I thought we left the porch light on," I said in surprise as David parked the car.

"We did," he answered.

"Then what's wrong?"

David climbed out of the car. "A blown-out light bulb, probably."

I stepped from the passenger side as he helped Jackie and a sleepy Stevie out of the Buick. We felt our way up the porch steps.

"I can't see a thing," I complained.

"You could wait," David said impatiently. "I'll have the lights on if you'll give me a minute."

"I'm a coward at heart," I admitted, pressing beside him.

As he put his hand on the doorknob and inserted the key, the door squeaked open. "Michelle, I thought you locked this door when we left." David was tired, almost reprimanding.

"I did," I said defensively. "So what's wrong?"

He pushed the door open cautiously, feeling inside for the light switch. With a flick of his wrist, the entryway flooded with light. We entered the house behind him. Suddenly I had an uneasy feeling that something was wrong.

"Oh, dear God, no!" Jackie exclaimed.

We followed her gaze to the spacious living area. The room was in shambles, ransacked. Table lamps were knocked over, books torn from their shelves. Ashes from the fireplace soiled the carpet; the contents of the hutch were spilled out on the floor.

Jackie ran down the hall.

David tried to warn her. "Wait, Jackie. Someone may still be in the house."

She never heard him. She raced to the kitchen. Stevie Jr. stood in the hall, sobbing in bewilderment. I scooped him up in my arms as we pursued Jackie.

"No . . . why . . . what do they want?" she cried.

She never waited for answers as she rushed from the kitchen, up the split-level stairway to the sleeping loft. Blocks, cars, and stuffed animals were sprawled across the floor. Candies were scattered on the dresser top. Stevie's Snoopy bedspread and matching sheets had been torn from the bed and draped over the antique rocking chair in the corner.

Jackie ran back down the steps to the northeast wing. We followed her into the master bedroom with its high, pitched ceiling and rough-hewn cedar walls. The room was a replay of the mess in Stevie's room. The glass door that opened to the rear sundeck and oval swimming pool was ajar. David went quickly over, slid the door shut, and locked it. Jackie was crying as she placed the pleated shade back on the bedside lamp. "Why? Why? Why!" she wept.

David gripped her shoulders. She kept sobbing. He shook her. "Stop, Jackie. Stop."

She reared back as though he had slapped her. "Why don't they leave me alone?" she screamed.

"Who?"

"They—they!"

"I don't understand," he said gently.

I doubted that she understood herself. "Jackie, I'm going to call the police," David told her. "But I need to know if anything is missing."

She looked around frantically, then made her way to the dresser through the clothes strewn on the floor.

"Your jewels? Valuables? Money?" David asked. "Where do you keep them?"

"Here," she answered, opening an Oriental jewel box.

"Is anything missing?"

She tried to focus on David. "My diamonds, my rings, my pendants—they're all here."

"You're sure?"

"I think so."

David glanced at the framed Degas print tilted on the wall. "Do you have a safe there?"

"No—not unless Steve had one is his office. He rarely allowed Stevie and me in there. Not after his friends started coming to the house."

"Show me Steve's office, Jackie."

She led us through the breezeway, down several steps to Steve's private office. David opened the door. We followed him inside.

Steve's office was the least disturbed of all the rooms. It was a masculine room with rich oak paneling and Spanish tiles on the floor. An old-fashioned rolltop desk was open, the contents dumped in a pile on top. Two roomy leather chairs with matching hassocks and a smoking stand between filled one corner of the room near the wet bar. On the other side of the room, the glass doors on the lawyer-style bookcases were ajar, but only a few books had been tossed aside.

David strode to the other side of the room and

checked the deadbolt on the outside door near the desk. Then he went to the phone, lifted the receiver and dialed the police. We heard him saying, "Yes, sir. I want to report a robbery—no, nothing seems to be missing. The house is a mess. No, of course not. No one is injured. But you see, there's been a recent death—" The control in his voice was growing thin. "Can't you send a squad car out this evening? Yes, the place has been ransacked. Someone was looking desperately for something. But who? And for what? We don't know. Thank you. We'd appreciate that. Yes, we'll wait up."

He slammed the receiver down and shook his head. "They'll be here within the hour. But it almost took an act of Congress." David leaned against Steve's desk and scanned the room. He mused, "It's as though the intruder knew this room—and had no need to really search it. . . ."

I had the same feeling. I looked at David and mouthed the word, *Steve?*

He shrugged, but there was a flicker of agreement in his dark eyes.

CHAPTER
TEN

The persistent ring of the doorbell roused me out of deep sleep. I opened my eyes groggily, wondering where I was. Then I sat up in Jackie's king-size bed. She hadn't stirred. Little Stevie was cuddled beside her, his stuffed goose under one arm.

With a fresh twinge of panic, I remembered last night's robbery attempt, the ransacked house, and the endless hours of questioning by the two patrol officers. I glanced at the bedside clock: It was 8:00 A.M. From my few fitful hours of sleep I felt as if it were still the middle of the night. But sure enough, the late autumn sun was beaming through the window. And the doorbell was still ringing.

"I'm coming!" I muttered as I threw on my robe and traipsed to the door. I peered through the peep-hole. It was a man—a stranger. A sudden, irrational fear knotted my stomach. Could this be the robber returning? "What do you want?" I called haltingly through the door.

"I'm Investigator Joshua Kendrick," he said, flashing an identification badge. "I'd like to talk with Mrs. Turman."

With relief I unhooked the chain lock and opened the door. "Come in," I said, gesturing toward the living room.

Joshua Kendrick stepped inside. He was tall, large-boned, and athletic, with a ruddy, handsome face and aquiline nose. He was dressed in a navy-blue business suit, starched powder-blue shirt, and khaki raincoat. "Mrs. Turman?" he inquired.

"No, I'm Jackie's friend, Michelle Merrill," I explained. "I imagine you're here about the robbery. I don't know what else we can tell you that we didn't already say last night."

He frowned, his thin upper lip curling slightly. "Robbery? I don't know anything about a robbery."

"But aren't you a police officer?" I asked in alarm.

"No, I'm a DEA agent."

"What?"

He gave me a slow, reluctant smile, revealing perfect teeth. "DEA is short for Drug Enforcement Agency."

"Drugs?" I looked at him, perplexed. "What are you doing here?"

"I'm here regarding Steve Turman."

"Steve Turman is dead."

"Yes, I'm aware of the accident," he replied. "But I have a few questions for Mrs. Turman."

"She's asleep. I really hate to disturb her."

"It's extremely important, Miss Merrill."

"Jackie's been so upset. Perhaps you could come back after the funeral."

"There may not be a funeral," he declared in low, precise words. "Now would you please call Mrs. Turman?"

I excused myself and went for David and Jackie. David was already dressed when he opened his door. "There's more trouble," I whispered.

"What's up?"

"I don't know but it looks serious. Go introduce yourself to Mr. Kendrick while Jackie and I dress."

"Mr. *who*?"

"Kendrick. He's a Drug Enforcement agent, David."

"You're kidding!"

"Please, David, just go!"

Joshua Kendrick was standing politely talking to David when Jackie and I entered the living room minutes later. "This is Mrs. Turman," I said. "Jackie, Joshua Kendrick."

They exchanged uneasy greetings. "Sit down, please," Jackie said.

After taking the chair she offered, Kendrick announced, "I'm here about the accident."

"Did you find out something new?" asked Jackie, immediately alert.

"Yes," Kendrick said quietly, "but I'm really here to ask you a few questions."

"What about?"

"Have you been called in to identify your husband's body?"

Jackie stiffened. "No, they haven't permitted me to do that."

"They?"

"Seward Brothers Mortuary."

"They told us Mr. Turman was too badly burned," explained David.

"Have you considered asking for an autopsy?" Kendrick inquired.

Jackie looked at me in alarm. She was beginning to breathe rapidly. I reached over to steady her, and asked, "Do you think an autopsy is necessary, Mr. Kendrick?"

"Yes, I do." His eyes remained solemnly on Jackie. "There's no easy way to put this, but it's quite possible that the man who died in the accident was not your husband, Mrs. Turman."

"That's absurd," exclaimed Jackie. "It was Steve's Mercedes."

"I know it was your husband's car, but we have reason to believe another man was driving it."

Jackie brightened for the first time in days. "Are you saying my husband may still be alive?"

"It's possible." Kendrick paused. "A friend of mine, a Drug Enforcement agent, is missing. He was last seen with your husband."

"That doesn't make sense," protested Jackie. "Steve didn't know anyone like that."

"I know for a fact he did, Mrs. Turman. Our agency has been investigating a local drug syndicate for months now. My friend had infiltrated the ring and was about to reveal the key members. We suspect your husband was involved—"

"Steve? Involved in drugs?" Jackie began to wheeze audibly. "How can you come here accusing my husband of such a hideous thing?"

I took Jackie's hand. It was clammy. "Can I get you some hot tea?" I asked.

She shook her head, regaining her composure. "What proof do you have, Mr. Kendrick?"

"Cocaine was found at the accident site."

"That doesn't mean anything. Someone could have thrown it in the ravine."

"It was found in your husband's car."

Jackie pressed her temples in a gesture of disbelief. "It can't be. Steve was an insurance salesman. He worked day and night. He traveled a lot, but his office was right here at home. When would he have had time—? He didn't know anyone on drugs."

"His friends, perhaps?"

She shook her head vigorously.

"What about those who purchased insurance from him—his clients?"

"No," she insisted.

Stevie Jr. shuffled into the room in his Mickey Mouse pajamas, dragging his favorite blanket and his stuffed yellow duck. He climbed up into his mother's lap. She wrapped him in her arms and kissed the top of his curly head.

Kendrick frowned briefly at the interruption. "Please, Mrs. Turman, try to remember," he urged. "Did you ever meet any of your husband's clients?"

"Most of them went directly to Steve's office through the outside entryway."

Kendrick leaned forward, his dark brown eyes direct, scrutinizing. "Did any of his clients come by regularly?"

She thought a moment. "One young man came rather frequently."

"Did you ever talk with him?"

"Not often."

"But on occasion?"

"Yes, but I really didn't like him," she admitted. "He was an arrogant, social misfit. I felt like he looked right through me. It made me feel cheap." She rubbed her hands nervously. "But he liked Stevie. I don't know why, but he took to the child. He would bring small presents, candy mostly." She paused reflectively. "He struck me as a brutal man, but he was gentle when he romped with Stevie."

"Do you remember the man's name?" Kendrick asked.

She shrugged. "Ray...Roy...something like that."

Stevie reached up and patted his mother's cheek. "Uncle Roys, Uncle Roys," he chanted.

"Were there other clients you remember?" Kendrick asked.

"Yes. A Greek fisherman—a big, friendly fellow."

"What was his name?"

"Andy something."

The interrogation went on. "What did he look like?"

She half-smiled. "Like a fisherman—windblown and sunburned. He always wore a wool skullcap and heavy boots."

"Did he live around here?"

"I don't know, Mr. Kendrick. I never asked him. He spent a lot of time deep-sea fishing in Cabo San Lucas. Steve had the insurance policy on Andy's fishing vessel."

"Do you recall any more of your husband's friends?"

Jackie was tired, her thoughts obviously drifting. "What does it matter now?" she asked.

"A great deal," Kendrick answered. "We have reason to believe several of his acquaintances were vital connections in the drug-trafficking scheme we're investigating."

At the threatening tone in Joshua's voice, David broke in with, "Mr. Kendrick, are you in line making these accusations? After all, Mrs. Turman has been through a great deal these last few days."

"I'm sorry," the agent answered coolly. "I thought if we could get some leads, perhaps we could know for certain whether Mr. Turman is alive or not."

"You're only guessing at Mr. Turman's involvement," observed David—"taking a long shot in the dark."

Kendrick smiled wanly. "I believe Steve Turman is still alive. I thought Mrs. Turman would be glad..."

"Glad?" Jackie laughed shrilly. "I'd almost rather have Steve dead than what you're accusing him of!"

"Mr. Kendrick, if Steve Turman is alive," inquired David, "who died in his car?"

Kendrick winced involuntarily as he said, "My friend and colleague, Paul Mangano."

In a stunned whisper, David and I both repeated "Paul Mangano?" We exchanged horrified glances. Were we thinking the same thing? Was Steve Turman really the stranger at Meadowgreen Airport? Had he deliberately assumed a dead man's identity? Worse, could he have played some role in Paul Mangano's death? I had assumed Steve might be running away with another woman, but illegal drug-trafficking and a possible murder involvement were incredible, unthinkable!

Jackie interrupted my dark thoughts as she mused aloud, "Paul Mangano?" Suddenly she sat forward, alert. "Michelle, the ring! I wonder if the wedding ring the mortuary gave me could belong to Mr. Kendrick's friend?"

"I don't follow," said Kendrick.

"The ring from the mortuary. It wasn't my husband's ring. The initials on it were P.M."

Kendrick's eyes riveted on Jackie. "I'd like to see that ring, Mrs. Turman."

Jackie stood up with Stevie still in her arms. "I'll get it for you."

After Jackie and Stevie had left the room, David looked squarely at Joshua and said, "I have a feeling that Jackie—Mrs. Turman—is also under suspicion."

Kendrick offered a detached, professional smile. "Mr. Ballard, anyone associated with the Turman family is suspect."

I sat forward, appalled. "Are you including David and me?"

He avoided the question. "Have you known the Turmans long?"

"Since Thursday," David answered. "Michelle has known Jackie since college, but they hadn't seen each other in years."

"Neither of us ever met Steve," I added.

"Then I suppose you have nothing to worry about."

"But we do have some information for you, a possible lead," David offered.

Kendrick studied David with a shrewd, calculating eye. "Go on."

"On Thursday—the day after Steve's accident— we met a man at Meadowgreen Airport who claimed to be Paul Mangano." David paused to let the import of his words take hold; then he picked up Jackie's wedding album from the coffee table, opened it, and removed a photograph. "The man at the airport—the one who claimed to be Mangano—strongly resembled this picture of Steve Turman."

CHAPTER
ELEVEN

Joshua Kendrick telephoned much too early on Saturday morning. "How are you, Michelle?"

"Exhausted," I confessed. "We spent yesterday cleaning up from the robbery."

"Did you discover anything missing?"

"No. At least Jackie says nothing."

"Then, whoever it was, was looking for something in particular."

"Something he didn't find. He even ransacked my suitcase. And David's."

"If any item turns up missing, will you let me know?"

"Yes. Yes, of course."

There was a polite pause, then Joshua said, "Actually, I didn't call about the robbery."

"What then?"

"Are you going to the mortuary today?"

"Later this morning."

"I'd like to accompany you. After what David told me about Steve Turman, it's urgent that we positively identify the body—"

"Then you're going in an official capacity?"

"No, I'll be going as a friend of the family."

"But you aren't—"

"I know. But it's important that we keep this investigation quiet. Shall I be there about ten?"

"I suppose so," I agreed. "Perhaps David could stay with Stevie. But I don't know how I'll explain this to Jackie . . ."

Drolly Joshua replied, "A bright gal like you will think of something."

But I didn't feel the least bit bright later that morning as Joshua drove Jackie and me to Seward Brothers Mortuary in San Luis Obispo. In fact, I felt overwhelmed with guilt. Jackie still didn't know about the man I'd met at the airport who bore such an uncanny resemblance to her husband. Nor did she know how David and I had implicated Steve more deeply in wrongdoing by sharing our suspicions with Joshua Kendrick.

Jackie said little during our drive. And she remained noticeably subdued a half-hour later when we walked through the flower-filled vestibule to Zachary Seward's office. I sensed her discomfort as she introduced Joshua as an old family friend. Seward put down his cigarette and affably extended his right hand.

Joshua ignored the hand and got right to the point. "Mrs. Turman has asked me to identify Steve's body, since you seem to have some reservations about her emotional reaction."

Zachary Seward planted his elbows on the desk and pressed his fingertips together. "That is an odd request, Mr. Kendrick, especially since Mrs. Turman ordered the body cremated."

I looked at Jackie. Her face went white. "But I didn't," she protested.

Mr. Seward retrieved his cigarette from an already-brimming ashtray, then gestured toward an official paper on his desk. "On the contrary, Mrs. Turman. You signed the authorization yourself yesterday afternoon."

Joshua glared. "Mr. Seward, are you saying—?"

The mortician nodded. "Mr. Turman's body was cremated early this morning."

"Oh, my God, no!" Jackie wheezed, her neck muscles contracting. "I didn't sign anything!"

"Of course you did," argued Seward darkly. He blew a circle of smoke in her direction. "You came back here alone yesterday and made the arrangements."

"Did you, Jackie?" I asked. "You *were* gone awhile."

"No, Michelle," she cried, her breathing labored. "I tried again to see Steve's body, that's all!"

"I'm not accusing you, Jackie," I said quietly. "I just don't understand."

Jackie coughed several times—a dry, tight bark. Then she clutched her chest, frantic. "I—I can't breathe—"

Zachary Seward pushed back his chair in alarm. "What's wrong with this woman?" he demanded.

"She looks like she's having a heart attack."

"It's her asthma," I said, going to her. Jackie leaned forward, her lips parted as she sucked desperately for air. "She can't tolerate the smoke and flowers," I cried. "She needs fresh air!"

Seward waved his hands wildly. His voice erupted in a high, startled croak. "Get her out of here, please! I won't have someone dying in my mortuary!"

Effortlessly Joshua swept Jackie up in his arms. "Come on, Michelle. There's a hospital near here."

In the car, I held Jackie against me all the way, as if she were my own desperately ill child. I watched helplessly, wiping perspiration from her face. Her nostrils flared and her dry lips turned a frightening ashen-blue. My prayers bombarded heaven for the first time in months as I bargained silently with God for her life.

Moments after Joshua pulled into the emergency entry at Sierra Vista Hospital, a nurse whisked Jackie away in a wheelchair. Joshua promptly telephoned his agency; I called David to assure him we'd be home as soon as we knew Jackie's condition. But Joshua and I waited for over an hour in the emergency room lobby before the doctor emerged and said, "We've decided to admit Mrs. Turman."

"It is that serious?" I asked.

"She hasn't responded well to the medications," he replied. "It's likely her husband's death aggravated her asthma."

"When can I see her?"

"It may be an hour or so before she's settled in her own room. If you'd like some lunch, the cafeteria is open."

Minutes later, after filing through the tray line, Joshua and I found an empty table in the noisy room bustling with men and women in white. As we sat across from each other, I had my first chance to really see Joshua Kendrick. He was a darkly handsome man, sinewy and muscular, with a shock of chestnut hair brushing his forehead. His brown eyes held a certain cynical expression—piercing, scrutinizing, direct. I had the uneasy feeling that he knew more about me than I wanted him to know. Yet, as we sat and talked, I found myself strangely drawn to him. He possessed a sensitivity, a trace of vulnerability I hadn't noticed during our earlier, official conversations.

Finally I broached the question that was plaguing me. "Do you think Jackie ordered the cremation?"

"I honestly don't know, Michelle." He glanced at his watch. "As soon as things are settled here, I'll return to my hotel to talk with my men about this latest turn of events." He paused. "Don't worry, I'll get you home too, after our brief detour."

"I'm more worried about Jackie," I conceded. "I can't believe she would deliberately do anything wrong."

"You're a very loyal person, Michelle. I admire that in a woman."

"But you think my loyalty is misplaced, don't you?"

His slow, reluctant smile revealed perfect teeth. "I believe a woman in love can be persuaded to do things that might surprise even herself."

"Are you speaking from experience, Mr. Kendrick?"

"Call me Josh," he said. "I haven't been fortunate enough to elicit such loyalty, Michelle. But perhaps someday . . ."

"Are you married?"

"Divorced. My wife couldn't handle the dangers and demands of my profession. I can't blame her. She wanted a secure life—a full-time father for our two boys, Juddy and Jon."

"I understand your wife's concern for your safety. Pursuing drug dealers must put you on the firing line every day. From what I've read, drug abuse is a growing problem in our country."

"A problem of epidemic proportions, Michelle. Cocaine alone is a 30 billion-dollar-a-year business. Over 24 million Americans have tried it. If it were rated as a legitimate industry, it would be considered number nine among American corporations."

"Josh, I had no idea it was that widespread!"

"Few people do. Coke is lethal, addicting. It's the second-greatest drug problem, next to alcohol."

I sighed, overwhelmed by the enormity of it all. "You certainly have your work cut out for you. How do you know where to begin?"

"We investigate every lead. Fortunately we have an international network of informants. We rely heavily on them and on undercover agents to gather evidence that will hold up in court."

"Didn't you say your friend, Paul Mangano, was an undercover agent?"

"Yes. He infiltrated this West Coast operation, but we still have no idea who the linchpin is."

"You don't suspect Steve Turman of being the leader—?"

"No, Michelle, but we hoped he would provide some good inroads. Until Paul disappeared, I really thought we were nailing it down."

"I thought most cocaine-trafficking occurred in Florida."

"It did, until Federal crackdowns started closing

operations there. Now they're coming in droves to the West Coast. Los Angeles could become the next cocaine capital of the world."

"That's incredible," I said, my writer's mind whirling with possibilities for stories. "But who are *they*...and where are they coming from?"

Josh drained his coffee cup. "The narcotics are smuggled from Colombia and other Latin American countries. Organized crime is involved, of course, but we're encountering more and more middle-class professional people and businessmen motivated by greed and the promise of big bucks. A kilo of cocaine wholesales in South America for 15,000 dollars and resells here for 65,000. If it's cut with another substance, such as baking soda or baby laxative, it sells for a whole lot more."

"How in the world do they smuggle it in?" I asked.

"Every way imaginable. And then some. They smuggle it on ships—freighters, pleasure craft, commercial vessels. Forty percent enters the country on private planes landing on remote airstrips. Whether drug-runners come by boat or plane, California's extensive coastline and massive desert terrain make it all too easy for them."

I shook my head, marveling. "The more I hear about your work, Josh, the most I respect you."

He smiled appreciatively. "You know, I could talk with you all day, Michelle, but we'd better get up to Mrs. Turman's room."

I nodded. We walked in contemplative silence from the hospital cafeteria to the medical wing. Joshua waited outside the door while I slipped quietly into Jackie's room. She was resting easier now, but her lusterless complexion matched the bleached bed linens. The head of her bed was elevated, the rails up. Her arms lay limp at her sides as a medication bottle dripped slowly into one wrist.

As I approached, Jackie looked at me with drowsy eyes and offered a flicker of a smile. "I guess I really messed things up this time," she murmured.

"Not quite as bad as during our good old popcorn days," I quipped.

But I couldn't get even a chuckle out of Jackie. Her face was etched with anxiety as she uttered, "You do believe me, Michelle. I didn't do it..."

"Do what?" I asked warily.

"Sign the paper. Mr. Seward lied..."

I leaned over the siderail and squeezed Jackie's free hand. "It's okay, Jackie. I—I'm praying for you. You rest now. The doctor said he gave you something to help you sleep."

"Stevie...?"

"Don't worry. I'll take good care of him. And you'll be home again before you know it."

My thoughts were still on Jackie during our 20-minute drive back to Morro Bay. Joshua followed Main Street, winding through a residential area to Morro Bay State Park. He pulled to a stop before the sprawling, scenic Golden Tee Resort Lodge.

As he climbed out of the car, he said, "Come on, my room's on the ground level facing the bay."

I hesitated. "Will we be long? I should call David."

"Call him from my room," Joshua offered.

"You won't need the phone?"

"No. My business matters require a personal contact." He unlocked his door for me. "I won't be long."

I felt vaguely uncomfortable alone in Joshua's

room. His personal effects were strewn across the empty bed; an open briefcase occupied the chair nearby. Some loose change and framed snapshots of his two sons were on the dresser. I studied their innocent, upturned faces as I dialed David.

"Turman residence," he answered brusquely. "David Ballard speaking."

"David, it's Michelle."

"Where are you? It's late. I've been worried."

"I'm in Joshua Kendrick's motel room." I regretted my words at once.

"I see," David answered, his voice restrained. "Is Jackie with you?"

"No, she's in the hospital for a few days."

"Then you're alone with Mr. Kendrick?" he asked coolly.

"Yes. . .no. . .I mean, Joshua just stepped out."

"Oh, it's Joshua now, is it?"

"Listen, David, I've got to go, but I'll explain everything when I get home."

An hour later I slipped out of Joshua's room and wrapped my sweater around me against the brisk October chill. I walked to the water's edge to await Joshua's return. To my left, the Blue Heron Rookery was shadowed among towering eucalyptus trees. Before me, spanning the darkening bay, bevies of sleek yachts bobbed at their floating docks. In the distance, the first mist of evening clung eerily to Morro Bay Rock.

I shivered in the vermilion twilight. Where was Joshua? Had he forgotten me? Did he care? Did anyone care? I felt suddenly lonely—and desperately alone. It struck me unnervingly that, ever since Scott. . .since my bitterness against God, I had been empty. There was a void within me waiting to be filled. Puzzling. Were my yearnings focused on man, or God—or both? As I stood openhanded in that wind-washed dusk, I sensed, in a singular moment of clarity, an approaching solstice of the soul, a turning point in my life. I would not pass through these days unchanged. It was a stunning, sobering realization—a crystal vision as fragile and fleeting as the plumes of mist feathering Morro Bay Rock.

Shortly after dark Joshua returned, offering no explanation for his long delay. He hurried me into his automobile and remained wordless for the brief drive to the farmhouse. I didn't mind. I wasn't in the mood for conversation either.

"I apologize for being so preoccupied," he said at last, as he escorted me up the walk to the porch. "It's just this whole baffling investigation . . ."

I nodded. "You're worried about your friend, Paul Mangano. It must be terrible not knowing whether he's dead or alive."

Joshua squeezed my hand appreciatively. "I hate to rush off, Michelle, but I must. Frankly, I may be onto something. I need to get back to San Luis Obispo at once." His voice took on a surprisingly intimate tone as he continued, "I hope I'm not out of line, but I'd like to see you again sometime soon."

I looked up, startled. "I—I'm sure we will. I'll be anxious to hear more about the investigation."

"Yes, that too." Joshua didn't wait for me to open the door. He was already striding back to his vehicle.

I rummaged in my purse for Jackie's key and entered the house with a sudden rush of relief and exhaustion. I wanted nothing more than to collapse into a hot tub and then into bed, until I caught the tantalizing aromas of baked potatoes and broiled steak. No, there was something more—a thick pungency in the air—something burning! I ran to the kitchen and found David leaning over the broiler amid billows of black smoke. With a chef's mitt he gingerly retrieved the thick, charred mass of sirloin.

"David, what are you doing?" I cried.

He squinted up at me through the dark haze, his expression a smoldering portrait of consternation, and snapped, "Cooking."

I grabbed a pot-holder and helped him carry his burnt offering over to the sink. "What happened, David? Didn't you time it?"

The charcoal-crispy slab sputtered and sizzled as it hit the wet stainless steel basin. David was sputtering too. "It wasn't the steak I miscalculated, Michelle. It was *you!*"

I ignored the insult and said testily, "I'm sorry your dinner is ruined."

David yanked several paper towels off the spindle. "That isn't all that's ruined, Michelle."

I stiffened defensively. "What do you mean, David? What else?"

His face slackened. "I mean the evening I planned for the two of us."

I stared incredulously at him. "Evening? The two of us?"

"All right, it was a dumb idea," he countered. "I figured you'd come home tired and upset over Jackie, so I was going to surprise you with a nice dinner. I got Stevie to bed early, and I thought you and I could..." his voice trailed off "...spend a quiet evening together."

"It's a lovely idea," I acknowledged. "Only...."

"You've eaten already?"

"Well, Joshua and I did have lunch at the hospital cafeteria—"

"You two had enough time together for a seven-course banquet," he gibed.

"David, that's not fair!"

"Of course it's not fair! I don't feel rational and objective at the moment. I spent the day with a three-year-old, remember?" He turned on the faucet and put his right thumb under the running water.

I reached for his hand and examined it. "You burned yourself on the platter."

"Just third degree," he muttered.

I looked up at him. "That isn't all that's burned."

"I know. I did a pretty good job with the sirloin steak too."

"More than that. You're angry with me because I was with Joshua Kendrick today."

"That's ridiculous!"

"Then why are you punishing me now, making me feel like I've done something wrong?"

"Because I've spent the day pacing this house waiting for you to come back," he exclaimed, "and I haven't been able to think about anything or anyone else but you!"

We were standing just inches apart, David's burned hand still in mine, the tension between us as thick as the charbroiled haze in the air. I was suddenly very much aware of David's physical presence, his brooding eyes searching mine, the near-warmth and solidity of his chest and torso. Then, in one swift, electrifying gesture he pulled me against him and brought his lips down on mine with an impassioned urgency that left me trembling.

CHAPTER
TWELVE

David released me with an expression of incredulity. I stepped back unsteadily, feeling light-headed, dazzled. "I hadn't planned on kissing you, Michelle . . .but it was wonderful."

"I—I enjoyed it," I admitted.

He raised a curious eyebrow. "Really?"

"Really."

He offered a sardonic smile and touched my cheek lightly. "I shouldn't have lost my temper with you earlier. I'm usually a very levelheaded man."

"I know." I reached up and put my hand over his. "And I forgive you for being jealous and angry."

His raw-umber eyes glinted shrewdly. "I didn't confess to jealousy."

I smiled. "And you had no reason to be. Joshua and I became friends today, but that's all."

David gently traced the contour of my chin. "I have no claim on you, Michelle."

I blinked with momentary disappointment. The sensation startled me. Was I actually hoping that David Ballard would stake some sort of claim—I who had spurned even the hint of a serious relationship since Scott? I turned away from David and remarked clinically, "I suppose that kiss was the result of the stress we've been through, an impetuous reaction to the tension of—"

David clasped my arm and whirled me around. "I kissed you because I wanted to. I wanted to know what it felt like to hold you in my arms."

"And—?"

He embraced me again, with a slow and careful tenderness. "It felt just right, Michelle," he murmured against my ear. "Warm and wonderful . . . and irresistible." His mouth moved over my face and neck to my collarbone.

I pulled away. "David, please . . . let's talk."

He raised his hands in exasperation. "I'm not managing this very well, Michelle."

"I know. Me neither. Suddenly the old rules don't apply. I—I don't know how to react to you, David."

"You can be yourself. I'll be myself."

"But I don't know who we are with each other. I don't want us to run headlong into a mistake."

"Is that what you think this is—the feelings we just shared? A mistake?"

"I don't trust feelings, David. They're too unpredictable. They can change . . . or stop."

"Don't you think I know that? I've been hurt too, Michelle."

"Then what are we doing, David, giving in to impulses that may be gone tomorrow?"

"I don't have the answer, Michelle...except that a part of me I thought was dead has come alive again with you, and it's a feeling I don't want to lose."

"I feel it too, David," I conceded, choosing my words carefully. "You've shown me I'll be able to respond to a man someday...when the time is right...and the right man comes along."

"Someday?"

"Yes, someday. I wasn't sure I could ever feel anything again after Scott."

"You're saying I cleared up that little question for you?" he asked ironically.

"Yes. And evidently I clarified the same matter for you. We can be grateful to each other for opening the door to new horizons—"

David tweaked my cheek. "You're babbling like an idiot, you know."

I shook my head in mortification. "Oh, David, I know I am. Why are you letting me rave on like this?"

"I know a cure, guaranteed to keep your lips occupied."

He advanced, eyes twinkling. I sidestepped him. "In this case, the cure may be more dangerous than the ailment," I cautioned.

He shrugged. I could sense he was retreating. "So what do we do now, Michelle?"

"We could clean the kitchen," I suggested, surveying the surrounding clutter.

David followed my gaze with obvious annoyance. "We haven't even had dinner yet."

"I'm a whiz with peanut butter and jelly," I volunteered.

An hour later David and I put the final gleaming touches on the stove and countertops. Everything was spotless again—just the way Jackie would want it. It was after nine when David and I carried steaming mugs of tomato soup into the family room and settled comfortably into oversized beanbags.

"I thought we were feasting on peanut butter," he mused.

"I changed my mind. Have you ever tried to sound fabulously scintillating with peanut butter stuck on the roof of your mouth?"

"So far I've avoided that rather sticky problem," laughed David. He looked over at the stereo. "I'd turn on some music if I could figure out how to get out of a beanbag holding a full cup of soup."

"No problem," I assured him. I set my soup on the plush carpet and artlessly propelled myself out of my concave leather nest. "Not too graceful," I admitted, "but at least we can sip our soup to music."

David and I sat in the semidarkened family room until midnight, talking confidentially to the mellow tones of Neil Diamond. Never had I felt so contented. Our earlier awkwardness had vanished as we shared bits of trivia about our lives, our childhoods, our choicest feats and foibles. In many ways we discovered that we were alike—both of us serious and absurd, stubborn and efficient, idealistic, private, perfectionistic.

"I'm very strict with myself," David disclosed. "I set up senseless little regimens just to prove I can adhere to impossibly demanding schedules. I like to feel in control at all times. I panic when I feel that control slipping."

"I'm exactly that way too," I agreed. "I don't let go easily. I suppose that's why I was so devastated by Scott. I had let myself be vulnerable with him. I had never been so open with anyone before, not even my parents or Jackie."

David nodded. "I was that way with Cheryl too. I thought I had finally found someone who really knew and understood me. I had mistaken her acquiescence for empathy. She never knew where I was coming from, and she didn't care..."

I studied David's shadowed profile. "And yet you aren't bitter—"

"I was at first," he conceded. "But, you see, it was because of my pain over Cheryl that I sought out God. I might never have sensed my greater need if it hadn't been for her."

"Isn't that merely rationalizing?"

One corner of David's lip curled in a perceptive smile. "You say that because you're still barricaded."

"What's that supposed to mean?"

"You insist on being invincible—to men, and I suspect, to God Himself."

"I believe in protecting myself," I said staunchly.

David absently massaged the scar that crisscrossed his jaw and said, "When I settled accounts with Christ, I realized I had to open all the doors and let Him see me as I was and accept me—vileness, weaknesses, and all. It was a humbling experience...and a glorious one. I realized He was the one Person I could be vulnerable with. I didn't have to erect barriers or manufacture glittering facades, like I often do with people. God took the raw, tarnished material of my life and transformed it into something He could use."

I smiled spontaneously. "If you had told me that last week, David, I'd have tuned you out."

"And now—?"

I sighed audibly. "Yesterday I prayed for Jackie, out of terror and desperation. Today I actually felt God for the first time in ages. He hasn't given up on me."

"Did you think He would?"

"I haven't been very lovable—"

"That was never a condition of God's grace."

I sat forward intently. "I want to find my way back, David. I really do." Tears welled suddenly; my throat tightened with an ache I couldn't verbalize.

"Come here, Michelle," David murmured.

Wordlessly I slipped out of my beanbag and settled beside David. He held me. I wept brokenly. He prayed over me with words I could scarcely hear. I could feel the emotion vibrating in his throat. Finally he said, "Amen." I tried to pray too. I could only get out, "I love You, Jesus." Then I heard David whisper, "I love you." I didn't know who he meant, so I sat quietly, my head against his chest, allowing my breathing to settle into a pleasant rhythm with his. We sat that way, hardly daring to move, for a long time. I wondered if he felt as I did—that we were one with God and one with each other in a way I had never experienced with another person. I didn't want to speak, lest the wonder of the moment shatter.

At last David leaned over and kissed me, not from the edge of passion but from a wellspring of tenderness. My mouth relaxed under his; my carefully contrived walls crumbled down around me. I was awash with roiling, rapturous emotions—love, joy, pain, anguish, ecstasy. I laughed and sobbed at once, while David kissed my tears.

Then I realized he was weeping too. "Why, David? What's wrong?"

"I'm still working through some healing of my own," he confessed, composing himself. "It hits me in rare moments when I least expect it. Like now, as I see you releasing your pain, it reminds me of my own. The truth is, usually we release our hurts guardedly, in small, measured pieces."

"Perhaps that's the only way we can handle them," I observed. Lovingly I traced David's scar along his jaw. "I can only speak for myself, David. My bitterness is gone. You helped me release it to God. I feel as new and clean as I did the day I walked the aisle to receive Christ as my Savior."

"I'm so glad, Michelle." His arms tightened around me reflexively, then relaxed.

I looked up into his eyes. "Will you tell me about that guarded bit of hurt you spoke of?" I urged.

He nuzzled my hair with his chin. "I mentioned it inadvertently when we were on the plane."

"You mean Cheryl?"

"No, not Cheryl. Vietnam." His facial muscles tensed slightly. His gaze moved away from me, beyond the room, to a place out of the reach of words.

"You told me about Eva's son Rob. He was your friend. You said you were with him when he died."

David's voice grew throaty, uneven. "I really haven't ever verbalized it, Michelle. I mean, I've discussed the surface facts—*what* happened, but not *why*. I've never laid it all out to anyone before."

"What do you mean, David?"

I felt his chest shudder involuntarily. "It's because of me that Rob died, Michelle. I killed him as surely as if I'd aimed my Colt .45 point-blank and fired."

I shifted so that I could draw his gaze back to mine. "I can't believe that's true, David."

"It's true," he said tonelessly. "You know, I've relinquished the guilt to God a hundred times over the years. Then one day I realize I've picked it up again, and the weight of it spoils my pleasure in Christ. I snatched it back again today. Maybe that's why I blew up at you earlier."

"What happened in Vietnam?"

David's words came slowly, gravelly. "Rob and I were flying our A-4 Skyhawk on an armed reconnaissance flight when we were shot down north of Hanoi. Somehow we both managed to crawl out of that broken hulk of a plane. I still remember how we laughed and cried and congratulated ourselves on saving our skins. Rob was removing our gear from the cockpit while I scouted for an opening through the brush.

"I had walked only a few feet from the plane when I spotted this boy—a kid maybe ten years old, if that. He was standing there half-covered by the underbrush, his black almond eyes staring at me from a gaunt, hungry face. That look went right through me. I stood motionless, my revolver poised. In that moment of indecision, of weighing alternatives, whether to kill or show mercy, that cherub-faced boy raised his hand and flung a grenade at our plane."

"How awful, David! What about Rob?"

David's voice was hollow. "There was nothing left of him."

"Oh, no . . ."

"I pulled off my shirt and held it against this gash

in my chin and ran blindly, stumbling through the spiky scrub, trying to find that boy. I wanted to tear him to pieces. Pure rage kept me going until my shirt was blood-soaked. Then the world started doing somersaults and I went blank."

"That's when you were rescued?"

"Correct. I was taken to a remote helicopter base in South Vietnam. I recovered physically in a few weeks. But I still see that kid—his eyes fixed and expressionless, hypnotic, boring into me. I see him in my dreams, on the street, in a dozen different faces of kids his age."

"David, you were brave to survive such a harrowing experience."

"No. Not brave. I did what I had to do . . . and I have to live with the fact that it wasn't enough."

"You can't know that, David."

"It wasn't enough for my friend Rob. Maybe he'd be alive today if I'd fired my gun."

"But you—you couldn't shoot a child."

"That's what I tell myself. But in a sense, there were no children over there. You never knew who your enemy was. The most innocent, dimple-cheeked youngster could be a trap. It was hell on earth, Michelle. Still, I've played it over in my mind a thousand different ways, and I always come back to the same bottom line: I couldn't shoot a kid."

"But you still wonder—?"

"Yes. I wonder whether I didn't shoot because of my high regard for human life . . . or because of my own cowardice."

"Never a coward, David," I soothed. "You couldn't be if you tried."

David wound a strand of my russet hair around

his finger. "I appreciate your vote of confidence, Michelle. You know, it just occurred to me—"

"What's that, David?"

He smoothed back the curl. "I realize tonight how guarded I've been with people. I think my experiences with Cheryl and the Vietnamese boy made me especially wary. I automatically scrutinize everyone to see if they're trustworthy."

"That's not necessarily wrong," I offered.

"No, but it's a barricade I've erected to keep people at arm's length. I haven't let anyone get close to me since Cheryl, just as you've kept men at a distance since Scott."

"But you've changed that for me, David," I confided. "I want to be open to love—God's love . . . and man's love."

"This man's love," David whispered, lifting my chin to his. He kissed me with warm, ardent lips. "I could hold you in my arms like this forever . . ."

I pulled away reluctantly. "David, common sense tells me we'd better call it a night."

"All right, but there's still tomorrow, Michelle. We'll spend it together, do something fun with Stevie." He thought a moment. "How about the Morro Bay Harbor Festival?"

I nodded dreamily. "Anywhere with you, David. Anywhere at all."

CHAPTER THIRTEEN

I woke frequently that night, feeling mellow and marvelous. My autumn dreams possessed a certain weightless exuberance, a romantic coppery hue. David and I were running toward each other in slow motion. Joyously he caught me in his arms. At his touch I felt a quiver of excitement. I luxuriated in the scent of his cologne as he held me, his lips seeking mine, my own responding. I kept thinking, *This can't be happening—me falling in love with the enchanting, elusive David Ballard.*

Before the first rays of dawn, I got up and showered. I was too distracted to sleep any longer. I dressed carefully with David in mind—a hunter-green blouse with its stand-up Pierrot collar, my brown corduroy skirt and camel blazer. I took a final glance in the mirror. The blouse was right—it brought out the gray-green of my eyes, and the natural blush in my cheeks highlighted my ivory complexion. Hastily I blotted my lipstick, softening the color for David. I gave my auburn hair one final fluff and was pleased with its fiery tint of gold.

"Okay, David Ballard," I said softly, stepping into the hallway. "Enough of 'pomp and circumstance.' I'll see what last evening meant to you."

I tiptoed past David's room, going through the silent house to the living room. Stevie was curled on the sofa, asleep on his tummy, one well-worn corner of his favorite blanket dragging the floor. David—all six-feet-one of him—was relaxed in the swivel chair near Stevie, an open Bible in his lap.

David was wearing a burgundy sport shirt and matching slacks, his hair neatly combed, the morning light from the bay window casting a special glow on his golden-beige skin. Like David's inner character, his facial features were finely cut, from his high forehead—creased now as he read—down his slightly irregular nose, to his firmly set jaw and that jagged scar that held so much memory for both of us now.

I went to him. "David?"

He swiveled, quickly offering me a wide grin as he grasped my hand. "Good morning, Michelle." He gave me an approving glance. "You look lovely."

"You're up early, David. Stock reports again?"

"I just couldn't sleep."

"I'm sorry."

"You should be." He winked. "I couldn't keep you out of my mind."

"You too?" I placed an impetuous kiss on his forehead, then drew back, embarrassed.

He laughed at me. "I liked that. But you're right. We do need to pull away."

His words startled me. "Why?"

"It's not what you think, Michelle. Last night is still very real and dear to me. I haven't changed. I love you. But . . ." David seemed to be choosing his words with care, "an isolated farmhouse on a lonely road, away from everyone else . . ."

He stood up and ran his fingertips along my arm. "I'm human, vulnerable. Last night I wanted to go to you in a way I've never wanted to go to another woman. Apart from the grace of God and my commitment to Him, I would have sought you out."

"I'm sorry, David."

"For my temptation?"

"For my own."

He nodded, understanding.

Stevie stirred, stretching on the sofa, calling for Jackie.

"I'd better give him his bath and dress him," I said.

"Michelle, I wouldn't mind getting Stevie ready myself. I'm catching a pleasant glimpse of what it would be like to have a wife and child of my own."

I smiled, pleased. "Then I'll get breakfast."

He caught my hand. "You're dressed too nicely for the kitchen. Why don't we make it a full day at the Harbor Festival. Breakfast and all?"

"Mommy?" Stevie was off the sofa, whimpering, shuffling toward the hallway. "Mommy?" he repeated pitifully.

David squeezed my fingers, then strode to Stevie, scooping him up in his arms. David turned back to me momentarily. "Why don't you call the hospital? See how Jackie is. Tell her our plans."

I had no sooner finished my call to the hospital when the phone rang. Thinking it was Jackie calling back, I grabbed the receiver and said breathlessly, "Hi. What'd you forget?"

"Good morning, Michelle," Joshua Kendrick's deep voice responded. "You sound out of breath."

"Josh, I—I was expecting Jackie," I stammered.

"Sorry," he laughed. "I won't hold you long. I was just wondering if you would care to have lunch with me here at the Golden Tee? They're having a Jazzfest. Or we could take in some festivities in town."

I hesitated. "I've already made plans for the day, Josh. I'm going to the Harbor Festival with David."

"Some other time perhaps?" He sounded wounded. He didn't wait for my answer but went on, "I guess it'll be business as usual. I've got enough paperwork to set up my own office here in my motel room."

"Thanks, Josh, for thinking of me."

"Don't thank me, Michelle. It's easy thinking of you."

As I replaced the receiver, I mused how flattered I would have been by Joshua's attention if David hadn't just come into my life.

At 9:00 A.M. David, Stevie, and I left the farmhouse in Jackie's Buick and drove through the sloping, sunburnt California hillsides that flanked Atascadero Road. As we rode along, I told David about my conversation with Jackie. "She sounds better," I assured him. "They still haven't stopped the IV, but she wasn't wheezing, and her voice was brighter."

"When can we pick her up?"

"She doesn't expect her doctor until late afternoon. So we won't know until then." I cleared my throat. "David, I told her about last night."

"About us?" His brows arched.

"No, about what God is doing in my life. It seemed to touch her when I shared how Christ has taken away my bitterness." I could hardly swallow, talking of it now. "She asked me to pray for her."

"Did you?"

"It was a first for me, praying over the telephone."

"That's great, Michelle. It's been a rough few days for Jackie, but it sounds like God is getting her attention."

I looked down at Stevie between us, clutching his little yellow duck. Then I said confidentially to David, "Jackie told me Joshua was there last evening."

"Kendrick? Why?"

"I'm not sure. I don't think Jackie is either, but she's afraid she's high on his suspect list. And she mentioned something else."

"What?"

"She sounded certain—she wasn't rambling." I hesitated. "But she really does think Joshua has DEA agents posted at her door. Can he do that?"

David sped another mile or two in silence, past golden fields and patches of trees and thick grass where Black Angus cattle were grazing. We were just passing the Rancho Colina Mobile Court on our right when he finally said, "We'll ask Joshua—tonight, after we get back. For now," he tousled Stevie's hair, "we're going to zero in on having the best day ever. If it's okay with you, we'll begin with breakfast at Dorn's."

Dorn's Breakers Cafe, a picturesque sky-blue, sat on a lushly verdant bluff overlooking the Embarcadero. As we entered the restaurant, I noted the tantalizing aromas of bacon, fresh biscuits, and home-brewed coffee. The clean, compact room was already crowded, bustling with local residents, tourists, and busboys in navy-blue aprons. One side of the room was decorated with blue-flowered wallpaper, punctuated by ancient lanterns and historic photos of Morro Bay.

A waitress led us to a small table where bay windows stretched across the dining room. The sun cut across the water and distant morning mist clung to the bottom of Morro Rock. Down by the waterfront, tourists were already milling in and out of Rose's Restaurant and peering in the shop windows of the Southern Port Traders. My gaze took in the *Hornet*, high in dry dock near the Galley Restaurant, then followed the black-and-white *B.J. Thomas* fishing vessel as it glided into port. The rest of the pleasure yachts and fishing boats bobbed in the water—bright ribbons, banners, and flags waving from their decks.

Far out by the man-made breakers, ocean waves splintered against the rocks, crashing, spiraling in sudden geysers, then collapsing in rolls of foam back to sea. Inside the breakers, the water rippled with a peaceful, lapping rhythm. I was eager to be done with breakfast, to be down on the Embarcadero browsing in the shops, walking hand-in-hand with David.

When the waitress finally returned, David ordered for us both. "How about some of Dorn's famous buttermilk pancakes along with their bacon and eggs?"

"Oh, David, the calories!" I protested.

He winked. "I'll finish what you don't eat."

The waitress nodded at Stevie. "What does your little boy want?"

David gave me a sly smile, then looked at Stevie. "What about it, Tiger? Hot chocolate? Strawberry waffle?"

I glanced out the window, embarrassed by my sudden pleasure at our being taken for a family. When the waitress walked away, David whispered to me, "It looks like we make a rather handsome family, wouldn't you say?"

Later, as David paid the cashier, she pleasantly rattled off a list of local sights we shouldn't miss. "Be sure to catch the yacht club races and the sand-castle-building contest."

"I wish there was some way we could see it all in a single afternoon," David told her.

"Well, you can get a great view of Morro Bay if you take a harbor cruise on the Tigers Folly stern-wheeler. And your son will love the Morro Bay Aquarium and Gift Shop." She smiled down at Stevie. "The Aquarium has lots of toys and real live seals."

As we left the restaurant, David clasped Stevie's hand. "Come on, Tiger." The two ran down the Centennial Stairway that led from Dorn's Restaurant to the corner of Front Street and Embarcadero. They were flying ahead of me, Stevie's feet barely touching the steps, his childish voice squealing in delight.

I followed, taking the wooden steps cautiously, my hand gripping the slippery metal railing all the way down. By the time I reached the last step, David and Stevie were standing breathless in the middle of the Giant Chessboard Square. David pointed to the sign, NO PETS WITHOUT A LEASH. "Oops, Stevie, we've got to scoot out of here or your duck will be in trouble."

"My goose," Stevie corrected, clutching the well-hugged animal.

"Where to first?" David asked. "We still have an hour before we catch the Tigers Folly cruise."

"Shopping, of course." I pointed to the brown building across the street—Southern Port Traders—and another two doors away.

David took my hand. "Just like a woman. Souvenirs first. Want anything special?"

I wanted to say, *I've already got someone special with me right now.* Aloud I said, "Maybe something to cheer Jackie."

In spite of his teasing, David was the first to make a purchase. Inside Port Traders, he found a brass, handcrafted model of an old sailing ship. He held it, inspecting it from stem to stern. "I'd like this for my office." He turned to the saleslady. "Can I have a name imprinted in the bow? And can you mail it home for me?"

"Yes, of course. And what name did you have in mind?"

David stole a glance my way, smiling. "How about 'Michelle's El Morro'?" While David made arrangements, I jotted down descriptions of the shop in my writer's notebook.

Inside the gift store two doors away, I told David, "I'd really like something to remind me of Shakespeare."

"In here?" he asked, his eyes taking in rows of the exquisite and the tourist-trivial, the fancy jewelry and the plastic toys. He boosted Stevie to his shoulders and wandered down one aisle. "Perhaps you'd better settle for this." He held out a hand-painted, balsam-wood carving of a sea captain, fully attired, with a peg leg, and a pipe in the corner of his mouth."

"Not exactly Shakespeare."

"Close. You could call him Captain Bill."

I picked up another carving—a seaman in thick black boots, yellow raincoat, and rubber hat with a weather-worn expression. "And I'll call this one Macbeth."

David leaned close and whispered, "I was afraid you'd call him David." His eyes held mine yearningly.

Along with our two carved seamen, the clerk wrapped a delicate china bud vase for Jackie. "We'll get Stevie a toy later at the Aquarium," David said as we rushed to catch the harbor cruise.

Twenty-five minutes later we leaned against the railing of the paddlewheeler as the Tigers Folly II pulled away from the Harbor Hut dock. Feeling the unsteadiness beneath my feet, I said, "David, do you think I'll get seasick?"

"No guarantee," he teased. "But the water looks calm."

"Not out there," I countered, pointing toward the breakers.

The Tigers Folly II was a 64-foot, shiny-white vessel, trimmed in blue, with an American flag

snapping from its stern. Sun rays streaked the surface of the water like fool's gold glittering in a
stream as we turned slowly and cruised along the
shoreline. Giant eucalyptus trees with their long
droopy leaves and fresh, pungent, cough-drop odor
lined the residential area.

The harbor was full of commercial and party
boats, fishing vessels, Coast Guard cutters, and
patrol boats. People waved and shouted. Seagulls
scolded. David ushered Stevie and me to seats
inside the cabin. Through the windows we saw
Morro Rock looming from the shorebed at the
hazardous bay entrance where erratic winds gusted
the rock.

Close up, the rock was dusty brown and barren,
scathed and buffeted by the surging tides of the
powerful Pacific. I braced my feet against the deck
of the ship. "We're not going out there, are we,
David?"

He laughed. "I don't think so."

"This feels like your Beechcraft Bonanza bounc-
ing against the winds, coming in for a crash landing."

He squeezed my shoulder consolingly. "Don't
worry. This boat trip should be placid by compar-
ison."

Nevertheless, I was relieved when the Folly turned
back from the rock. As we wound along the calm
waters by the Embarcadero, we tried to spot frolicking sea otters and waterfowl, but all we saw were
more boats. *The Sea Ranger. The Anabella. The
Bonnie Doon.*

Suddenly, as a sloop with a royal blue sail cut
across our path, Stevie pointed and cried excitedly,
"Daddy's goose. Daddy's goose! I wanna see Daddy!"

"What?" I asked, puzzled.

"It's gone now," Stevie fretted. "You didn't stop."

"We can't stop, Tiger," David answered. "We're on a big boat."

Tears streaked Stevie's face as he cuddled against David. "I want my daddy."

"What's he talking about, David?" I asked. "What did he see?"

"The same thing we saw. A hundred pleasure boats on Morro Bay." David lifted Stevie onto his lap and rubbed his forehead soothingly. Moments later, the child was asleep.

CHAPTER FOURTEEN

By 3:30 Stevie, David, and I were sitting on a log overlooking an inlet of water, munching a late lunch of fish and chips. We watched the fishing vessels making their way back to the launching ramps. Fishermen stood on the *Pacific Fin*, skillfully filleting the day's catch with wood-handled knives. A crooked sign on the cabin window read: TUNA FOR SALE. On the *Billie G.* nearby, the men stood in rubber hip boots, reeling in their huge nets. Seagulls skimmed the water, circled the vessels, then hovered above them, squawking for fish scraps.

"This has been a long day," David said at last.

"I think we'd better get Stevie home to bed."

Stevie pouted, "I want my toy first."

"That's right, Tiger. We promised you a trip to the Aquarium way back at breakfasttime. But after that we head to the hospital for your mommy, then home."

"I want my mommy and daddy," Stevie whimpered.

"I know," David answered as we headed for our final shopping spree.

The Aquarium and Gift Shop, with its garish green sign and windows displaying colorful imprinted tee shirts, was an earthtone building on the southern end of the Embarcadero. Behind the store a rocky ledge led down to the bay, where several small boats were moored. As we strolled to the front of the shop, we heard the hoarse, grating bark of the harbor seals and sea lions. Stevie shrank back in the doorway. "I'm scared. I want to go home!"

"That's ridiculous. You want to go in," David insisted. "They have toys in there. Fun things."

The seals barked again. "I'm scared of the monsters," Stevie persisted.

"The seals won't hurt you, Stevie," David said, growing impatient. "They're in the aquarium."

Stevie wouldn't budge. "You go. I stay here."

"But, Tiger, they have nice plastic cars and stuffed animals."

"David, you're arguing with a three-year-old."

"Then you handle it."

I grabbed Stevie's hand and marched him inside. His piercing protest rivaled the seals' irritating yelps. I ignored the icy stares of the milling shoppers and grinned sheepishly at David. "You grab a postcard for Eva and I'll pick out a toy for Stevie."

David headed down one narrow aisle, ducking under the sea-shell wind chimes, squeezing awkwardly through the throng of tourists. I glanced around. The shop was crammed from floor to ceiling with souvenirs, novelties, ceramic mugs, and stuffed toys.

"Stevie, would you like a fuzzy white rabbit?" I asked.

He shook his head. "No, I got my goose."

I frowned at the faded, stuffed yellow duck. "Then how about this Panda bear?"

Stevie looked away, rolling distractedly on his feet, then meandered down the aisle, running his stubby hand along the counter. "I want to go home," he mumbled again.

I pulled him back. "If you don't want an animal, how about a nice hat? Look, Stevie, this hat says Morro Bay. Do you want a red one or green one?"

Stevie tugged at my skirt. "Uncle Roys... Uncle Roys!"

I sorted through the hats, looking for one with perfect stitching. "Here, Stevie, try this one on." I turned and looked down. My heart lurched. He wasn't there. I looked up and down the aisle. "Stevie, Stevie, where are you?"

I tapped the arm of the squat, rotund lady beside me. "Did you see a little boy? A little blond boy in blue jeans..."

She shook her head, her rouged jowls shaking like Jell-O. "Try the Aquarium," she said pleasantly. "Kids love seals."

"Not Stevie!" I darted to the end of the aisle and found David at the cashier's stand. "David, where's Stevie?"

"You know I left him with you."

"He's gone!" I answered haplessly.

"Maybe he ran outside," the cashier suggested.

David pushed past the customers and scanned each aisle, then strode out of the store. I was close on his heels. He stopped and stared intently at the Shell Shop across the street, then down the sidewalk toward the Hofbrau Restaurant. He called Stevie's name over and over.

The cashier from the Aquarium shop bustled up to us. "I hope you don't mind. I took the liberty of calling the police. They're on their way."

"Thank you." David reached into his pocket, took out a slip of paper and handed it to her. "Call this number, please. Insist on talking to Joshua Kendrick. Tell him to meet David Ballard here at once."

She nodded and slipped back inside the store.

"David, the bay!" I cried, my voice choked with urgency. "What if Stevie fell in the water?"

Without a word David took my hand and ushered me along. A makeshift fence separated the rocks from the parking strip. The bay rippled gently at the bottom of the rocky slope. One boat slip was empty.

My eyes searched the craggy incline down to the transparent water, lingering on something yellow wedged in the rocks. David followed my gaze, then sprinted over the fence and scrambled gingerly down the slanting shoal. He leaned down, grasped the item, and held it up. It was Stevie's stuffed duck. At once David waded waist-deep into the bay, shoes and all. He moved through the water with silent determination. Three strangers— one in a wet suit—simultaneously bounded over the rocks and waded into the water with David.

They spread out, moving cautiously. The surfer dipped under the water, broke the surface several times, then dove again. He reappeared, shook the water from his tanned face, and called, "I can't find any youngster here!"

"Keep looking," I begged.

The man dove again.

A crowd was gathering—the curious, the concerned. Beside me, another stranger spoke consolingly. "Help is on the way. Someone sent for the Coast Guard patrol boats..."

A teenage boy with sun-bleached hair squinted up at me. "I'm telling ya, somebody just took off in a motor boat. In a real big huff."

"Was a little boy with them?"

"Dunno."

I gazed urgently out over the waters, as if staring would bring Stevie back into view. There were so many boats on the horizon. Was it possible Stevie was on one of them? The monotonous bark of the aquarium seal lions taunted me. I could hear the murmuring questions of the crowd gathering in the parking lot. The siren of an approaching police car blared shrilly. David, dripping wet, climbed back up the rocks to me. He handed Stevie's duck to me, then turned and walked back to the police vehicle.

Moments later I heard a police officer ask, "Aren't you the gentleman we met at the robbery on Atascadero the other night?"

"Yes, sir," David answered. "At the Turman residence."

"Trouble again?" the officer inquired.

"Yes, sir." David's voice was edgy. "The Turman boy is missing."

"I see. How long ago?"

"Ten—fifteen minutes ago."

"Can you give me a description of the child?"

"He answers to Stevie Turman. He's about 30 pounds, three feet...sandy brown hair, curly, and dark eyes, no, blue eyes. I don't know for sure."

"What was the child wearing?"

David cleared his throat. "Blue jeans. Yes, I'm sure. Blue jeans and sneakers...a pullover shirt, kind of light brown, and a blue denim jacket. I should tell you...he has trouble with asthma."

Their voices faded as I thought about Stevie, alone, frightened, perhaps even hurt or in danger. I clutched his cherished duck. The afternoon mist had already begun to blur the base of Morro Rock, creeping eerily up the jagged edges toward the rim. Ominous, black clouds were forming in the distance, hovering above the ocean, casting gray shadows over the fishing town. A foghorn blared warnings to fishing vessels beyond the breakers, still far from the safety of their moorings. "Oh, God," I cried, "please protect Stevie!"

"Michelle," David said gently. "Joshua Kendrick is here."

I turned and looked up at Joshua. He seemed restrained, his face weary, but he took my hand awkwardly in his. "Michelle, we'll find Stevie."

"Like you've unraveled the mystery of his father?"

I could see my words stung. "That too," he said determinedly. "I just talked to a witness who saw a boy fitting Stevie's description leaving in a motor launch." Joshua's face was cold as steel; his eyes piercing. "It looks like Stevie may have been kidnapped."

"Then he's in more danger than ever!"

"Not necessarily. His captors will need him to bargain with. They won't harm him until they get what they're looking for. That gives us time. . ."

"How much time?" asked David.

Joshua gazed solemnly at us. "David, Michelle, there's more you don't know. Not only do we have a missing child. . .but also a missing father."

"What do you mean?" David demanded.

"Our investigation of Seward Brothers Mortuary confirmed our suspicions. The cremation of Steve Turman never took place. It was a subterfuge to prevent Mrs. Turman from identifying the body."

I felt my legs buckling beneath me.

Josh went on. "In the last 48 hours there was another attempt to transfer the body from Seward Brothers. Only this time my men intercepted the transfer."

"You mean the Seward brothers are involved in this too?"

"Yes. We have them under surveillance."

"Surveillance?" David repeated. "Why don't you just pick them up?"

"We're going for the kingpin, David."

"And who's that?"

"We don't know. But we do know that the mortuary is not the center of activity." He half-smiled at his own droll humor. He turned to the two DEA agents who had just joined us. "Any trace of the boy?" he asked them.

"Negative," the taller one responded. He nodded toward the bay. "The Coast Guard patrol boats will handle that end of it. They'll be dragging. . ."

Joshua cut him off. "What about a vessel-to-vessel search?"

"Negative," the man said again. "What with the Harbor Festival, it's just about impossible."

"Joshua," David questioned, "if it wasn't Steve, who died in that accident?"

Joshua's mouth twisted painfully. "My friend, Paul Mangano."

"I'm so sorry," I told him.

David slipped his arm securely around my waist. "What about Steve?"

"It's possible he kidnapped his own son."

"That's absurd," I exclaimed.

"Not if you're fighting for your life. We know for a fact that Steve and Paul Mangano, our undercover agent, were acquainted, probably working together in the drug operation." Kendrick's brows arched, perplexed, as though he were wondering what to share. "Paul was trying to get information to us. Crucial information. He was coding a report. We never got it."

"Then someone else must have," David noted. "It's obvious the farmhouse was ransacked for something. Maybe your agency and the drug syndicate are after the same thing. The child may simply be caught in the middle."

"I've got to get to the hospital," I interrupted. "I've got to tell Jackie what's happened to Stevie."

"No," Joshua replied sharply. "I'll see Jackie myself. In fact, we'll keep her in the hospital for her own protection. You two go back to the farmhouse and stay there until there's contact from the kidnappers. If you hear from them—or if you hear from Steve—let me know at once. Whatever happens, let me handle it. I'll leave word at the registration desk at the Golden Tee. You can reach me there, day or night."

Joshua turned abruptly and walked with his men to the police car. David took my hand and led me back toward the car. As we walked, a silent crowd broke a path before us. The rouged, rotund customer from the gift shop reached out and patted my shoulder as we went by.

CHAPTER FIFTEEN

That evening after we had returned to the farm-house, David brought some bedding into the darkened living room. He dropped two pillows and a blanket on the sofa for me. "We'll sleep here by the phone," he announced.

"Sleep?" I stared at him in disbelief. "Maybe we'd better sit by the kitchen phone and drink coffee."

He took his own bedding to the recliner that faced the front window, then opened the drape slightly. "We can watch Atascadero Road from here."

I made my way over to him through the darkness.

He was staring intently at the cars passing down Atascadero. I watched the headlights of one vehicle dim and suddenly go out. I had an unsettled feeling that the car had turned into the Turman driveway. "David, I think we're being watched."

"No doubt. Kendrick would hardly risk having us here at the farmhouse alone."

"I didn't think about that. The only thing on my mind is Stevie."

David slipped his arm around my waist. "We have to believe that God is taking care of Stevie." He said it so fiercely that I wondered for a moment if he doubted it himself. I glanced up. The moonlight breaking through the clouds profiled David's face. His jaw was firmly set, his eyes unflinching.

I peered out again into the night and blinked. Was that the silhouette of a car behind the eucalyptus trees? I couldn't be sure. "David," I whispered, "what if it isn't Joshua's men out there? What if. . .?"

David drew me closer.

"I'm frightened," I confessed.

"We both are," he said evenly. "But we have a job to do."

"A job?"

"We're to wait for the phone to ring."

"How long do you think we'll have to wait?"

"We may be here all night. We can spell each other. I want you to go ahead and change, shower, whatever. Be dressed and ready to go at a moment's notice. I'll do the same."

It was 5:00 A.M. when the phone finally rang, rousing me out of a troubled sleep.

"Michelle," David said solemnly, stirring from his

chair, "you answer it. The kidnappers will be expecting Jackie."

I picked up the receiver, trembling. "Hello?"

A muffled, masculine voice said, "Michelle Merrill, if you want to see Stevie Turman alive, you'll do exactly as I say."

David pressed his head against mine, listening.

"Who are you?" I cried. "Is Stevie all right?"

"So far," came the cryptic response. "You have something we want. We plan to make a fair exchange."

"What? What do we have?"

"A key, Miss Merrill."

"What key? I don't know what you're talking about."

"I believe you do," he answered coldly. "A man at the airport gave you a key. We want it."

I frowned, trying desperately to remember.

"Go to the Chessboard Square. You'll find further instructions on the bench facing Dorn's Restaurant."

"I don't have any key . . ."

"The boy for the key, Miss Merrill." The line went dead.

I stared at David. "Key? Airport? He must mean Meadowgreen Airport."

"The stranger who bumped you—"

"Paul Mangano—?"

"No, Steve Turman." David paused, perplexed. "But I saw you give back the key, Michelle."

"No, David, I didn't. Steve insisted I keep it. He said something odd . . ."

"Where is the key?" pressed David.

"I dropped it in my purse. It must still be there. But I wish I could remember . . ."

"You had that purse with you the night the house was ransacked, didn't you?"

I nodded.

"Then check your purse, Michelle, while I call Kendrick."

When I returned a minute later, David was hanging up the phone. "Here it is, David," I said, holding up a gold medallion key chain. "What did Kendrick say?"

"I couldn't reach him. He was en route to the hospital, so I left a message with both the hospital and his hotel."

"You told *them* we heard from the kidnappers?"

"No, I just said we're going after Stevie at the Chessboard Square. We can't risk waiting for Kendrick. Besides, knowing him, he'll catch up with us."

"You mean we're going to give up the key, just like that?"

"What else can we do? Stevie's life is at stake."

"But it was Stevie's father who trusted me with the key," I reflected. "There had to be a reason."

As we walked out the door, David picked up Stevie's favorite stuffed toy that we had found on the rocks. He tossed it in the backseat as we got in the car. "Tiger will want his duck when we see him."

"His goose, you mean." I lurched forward as David's foot hit the gas pedal. "Oh, David, that's it. That day at the airport, Steve Turman said something about a goose!"

"What?" David was speeding down Atascadero.

"I don't remember—" I stared again at the key in the palm of my hand. The gold engraved letters "P.M." glinted back at me. The key was flat and thin—too large for a door. "Maybe this is Paul Mangano's mailbox key," I suggested.

"Mangano was transient," David answered. "He didn't have roots in Morro Bay. He was simply assigned here with the drug administration." David turned left off Atascadero Road, barely braking. He nodded toward the glove compartment. "There's a guidebook in there. Find out where the Morro Bay post office is. Mangano had to have a contact point somewhere. What better spot than a casual stroll in and out of a post office?"

Minutes later David pulled to an abrupt stop before the cream-colored building on Napa Street. He was out of the car before I could even open my door. I climbed out and ran after him into the post office. The mailboxes occupied a large section of the building. "Wow, where do we begin?" I asked, staring at the endless rows.

David took the key from me. "Nineteen-something. The number is partially scratched off." He looked around. "This is the 1900 section," he said, walking over and attempting to insert the key in the nearest box. He moved along steadily, row after row.

An early riser—a bewhiskered old gentleman—swung in through the doorway, eyed us curiously, then went for his mail. After he left, David tried again. On the third row from the bottom, the key turned. David opened the box and removed the contents. He slipped several cassette tapes into his jacket pocket, then hurriedly scanned a thick folder of papers. I peered over his shoulder at one handwritten document. Bold black words, ink-blotched and underlined, caught my eye. I smudged the words further with my forefinger.

"David, the *Wild Goose Chase*. What is it?"

"According to this, it's a sports fishing vessel moored here in Morro Bay." He shook his head. "I can't believe it. Names. Locations. Dates for cocaine transactions. There's enough evidence here to incriminate pivotal figures in a drug syndicate operating in this area and using the *Wild Goose Chase* for its smuggling."

"This must be the information Paul Mangano was trying to send to Kendrick," I said. "David, is Steve's name . . . ?" I couldn't finish.

He nodded sadly. "Steve's name is here." He folded the documents carefully. "We need to get these and the tapes to Kendrick. Do you have the hospital number?"

"Yes." I pulled out my writer's notebook. "There's a phone over there," I told David, pointing to the public booth by the flagpole.

As we left the post office, I noticed that the city of Morro Bay was waking now. A newsboy peddled by on his bicycle. A car whipped around the corner near where we stood. A bearded motorcyclist gunned his Honda. I dropped the coins into the slot and dialed the hospital in San Luis Obispo. As I waited for Joshua to answer, I said, "David, show me Steve's name on the document."

He removed the top sheet and handed it to me. "Steve's name is toward the bottom."

I put the paper on the phone ledge with my notebook and ran my finger along the maze of information. As I did so, I heard a distant voice say, "Kendrick speaking."

"Josh, this is Michelle."

"Michelle! Where are you?" His voice was curt, angry. "I told you to stay at the farmhouse."

"We couldn't, Josh. Believe it or not, we've just found out we're really on a wild goose chase—"

I felt cold metal slapped against my neck. "Hang up. Not another word," a harsh voice ordered.

"Do as he says," David told me.

I dropped the receiver. As it dangled aimlessly, I could hear Kendrick's muffled voice calling, "Michelle, Michelle. Answer me!" I reached to pick up my notebook, but a firm hand gripped my arm and pulled me from the booth. A familiar, ruthless face glared down at me.

"You're Royce Adams," I exclaimed. "The pilot from Meadowgreen Airport."

"You remembered," he said cockily.

"Uncle Roys. You're Uncle Roys!" I realized aloud.

"Get in," he commanded, pointing his .38 revolver toward the green Toyota at the curbside.

David took my hand in his. "Do as Mr. Adams says, Michelle. For Stevie's sake."

David squeezed into the car beside me. Royce followed, slamming the Toyota door shut. "Gun it, Andy," he said.

The driver, a big-boned man with a sunburned face and red wool skullcap, released the hand brake and shifted into drive. Our vehicle shot forward. We sped the few blocks down to the bay.

As we stepped out on the dock, I quelled the urge to run, to escape. David, perhaps sensing my terror, held my hand tightly. Royce and Andy walked behind us to the end of the pier, where a small blue sloop was tied. David stepped down the ladder first, then turned and lifted me to him. The men climbed in beside us.

As the skiff sailed from the pier, the sun reflected off Royce's revolver. His lips curled bitterly. "You two don't take orders very well," he said, tapping the Mangano papers he had taken from David. When we didn't answer, he persisted, "I told you, Miss Merrill, the key for the boy. You could have had the boy and gone free. But you had to snoop further."

As I watched Royce, I remembered Jackie saying, "He's an arrogant social misfit, but he likes Stevie." It was a glimmer of hope. If he liked the boy, perhaps Stevie would be safe.

David took my arm as Andy eased the sloop over beside a luxurious sports fishing vessel bobbing quietly at a floating dock in the middle of the bay. I followed his gaze. The name *Wild Goose Chase* flashed boldly, ominously from the bow.

CHAPTER
SIXTEEN

As David and I stepped on the floating dock, it swayed beneath us. Royce nudged us toward the rope ladder at the stern of the *Wild Goose Chase*, a sleek, white, maroon-trimmed vessel with a grandiose command station and seagoing veranda.

After we had scaled the ladder, Royce motioned us across the open deck and up the stairwell to the plush, teak deckhouse. We entered a spacious living area with oversized windows, golden carpeting, and elegant, ivory-colored furnishings. A six-foot, silver-blue sailfish graced one paneled wall. We passed a round dining bar to the L-shaped sofa. "Sit down," Royce ordered, twirling his revolver. "Make yourselves at home. But don't get any smart ideas about leaving. We have two crewmen on guard outside."

"Where's Stevie?" I asked, looking around.

"Below deck. With his old man."

"Then Steve Turman did kidnap his son!"

Royce's left eye winked involuntarily. "Wrong, lady. It was me. I said I'd take him to his daddy. A bag of candies and a nice little boat ride made his day."

"But why would Steve want you to kidnap his child?"

"He didn't have a choice in the matter," said Royce with an arrogant glare. "We needed Stevie to get to you...and the key."

"You have your key," I said. "Now let us have Stevie and we'll go."

Royce gave a quick, brutal laugh. "Too late, lady." He signaled to Andy in the open galley. "Bring Steve up, Skipper."

"Up here, Royce?"

"Yeah, it's safe. They're not going to try anything with little Stevie below deck." He glanced at his watch. "We're cutting it close timewise, but I'd better take the sloop ashore and contact the big boss. He's gotta know about this foul-up."

"We're still gonna make the run, aren't we?" asked Andy.

Royce nodded. "We'd better. This is the big one, man. No way I'm going to miss it."

"You and me both," said Andy. He went below deck and was back moments later with the man whose face had haunted me for several nights. Steve Turman was the same tall, slender man I remembered meeting, with handsome features and troubled, deep-set eyes. Those eyes bore through me now as we stood face-to-face, appraising each other.

"Michelle, I'm sorry," he told me, his voice a raw whisper. "When I saw you at Meadowgreen Airport, I had no idea you were Jackie's friend. I never would have involved you in this mess."

"Where's Stevie?" I demanded.

"He's okay. Asleep in the stateroom."

I tried to control my rage. "How could you have done this to Jackie!"

"Believe it or not, I did it *for* Jackie," he countered. "At least, that's how it started." He nodded toward the sofa. "It's a long story. Why don't we sit down?"

David glanced over at Andy in the galley. "What about him?"

"He won't bother us." Steve took the salon chair opposite the sofa.

"Well, you have a captive audience, Mr. Turman," David said gruffly, sitting down. "Would you mind telling us what's going on?"

Andy passed by with a steaming coffee mug. "The brew is fresh, mates, if you want some." His ruddy, leathered face crinkled in a bawdy grin. "Don't try nothin' foolish. I'll be just outside on deck."

As soon as Andy had gone, Steve leaned forward intently. "Tell me about Jackie. Is she all right? Does she think I'm dead?"

"She's devastated, sick. She doesn't know what to believe. She's in the hospital with her asthma."

Steve buried his face in his hands, shaking with such deep emotion that for a moment I almost pitied him. When he gazed up at me again, he looked like a broken man. "I love Jackie," he said. "And Stevie. I'd do anything for them, anything to protect them."

"If that's how you feel, why did you get involved in something as dangerous as drug-trafficking?"

"For the money, Michelle. From the time Jackie and I were married, I really worked hard. I wanted to prove I could provide even better for her than her parents had. She expected so much. But it was always a problem of too few insurance sales, too little money."

Steve's expression was desperate, intense. "Then two years ago I went deep-sea fishing just to get away. That's when I met Andy Watson, the skipper. He offered me some cocaine. I dabbled in coke a few times to give my sales pitch a boost, to gain some confidence. But I decided it wasn't for me. A few weeks later Andy introduced me to his friends, Royce Adams and Leon and Zachary Seward. At first Zachary said all I had to do was deliver a package or two, no questions asked. The payoff was incredible."

"You weren't curious about what the packages contained?" said David.

"Yes, but I needed the money. I was in too deep when I learned they were using my insurance connections as fronts for cocaine-trafficking. Then the syndicate offered me bigger money for the use of the farmhouse for their West Coast drug transactions. Money was pouring in for me. I kept figuring I'd pull out as soon as the farmhouse was finished and the bank account high enough."

Steve nervously twisted his wide wedding band. "But I got scared when a guy I knew died. Mike smuggled coke from South America by "body-packing"—carrying it in his body cavities. But the last time he swallowed the stuff. He was detained so long at customs that the packets must have come apart in his stomach. He died of a drug overdose before he even left the airport. What gets me is he must have known he was dying and never even said a thing."

"Was it worth his life?" I asked somberly.

"It would have been worth plenty, at 28,000 dollars a kilo."

"If Mike's death scared you, why didn't you get out then?"

"I was ready, but something else tipped the scales for sure." Steve's brown eyes smoldered. "A crackdown on the manufacture of cocaine in Colombia forced refiners to set up their clandestine labs in this country. When the syndicate wanted to turn a secluded area of my farmland into one of their highly explosive cocaine labs, I panicked. I didn't want uncut coke on the property, or the smell of ether permeating the neighborhood. And God knows I didn't want to risk an explosion so near to Jackie and Stevie. That's when I decided I had to get out of the ring."

"So you ran away, assumed another man's identity?" I asked. "How did that protect your family?"

"I had no choice, Michelle. Jackie and Stevie were in danger. Paul Mangano was already dead."

"You killed him?"

"No," Steve denied hotly. "Paul was my one chance to get out of this mess."

"Were you aware he was an undercover agent?" questioned David.

"Not at first. I thought he was another runner. We became friends. Then, a few weeks ago, I discovered he was with the DEA. I told him I wanted out and offered to turn state's evidence. Our organization was planning its biggest run of all—a rendezvous with a Colombian tramp steamer 200 miles at sea. Paul knew about the run, but I'm sure he was on to something even bigger. He said he was ready to crack the case wide open. He was going for the top man."

"Who is the top man?" asked David.

Steve shrugged. "I have no idea. It's not Royce, but I think he knows who it is. It could be Zachary or Leon Seward, but I think even they answer to someone higher."

"Paul Mangano must have known," said David.

"I'm sure he did." Steve's eyes clouded. "Last Tuesday, just hours before he died, Paul and I were to meet the Seward brothers in Cambria. Before we arrived, Paul gave me the key to his post office box. He told me he was sure someone was on to him. He said if anything happened to him I should deliver the key to his contact in Morro Bay."

"That must have been Joshua Kendrick," David offered.

"But, Steve, you gave *me* the key at Meadowgreen Airport."

"I had to, Michelle. It was my only chance of getting it into the right hands."

"But what happened to Paul Mangano?" David pressed.

Steve shook his head. "Everything fell apart last Tuesday. After our meeting, the Seward brothers took Paul away in my car. I had no idea why—until they and Royce returned hours later without him. They told me Paul was dead, burned beyond recognition at the bottom of a ravine in my car. They had discovered his undercover operation and, as they put it, had discreetly disposed of him. Leon said I was to assume Paul's identity and fly out from Meadow-green Airport as soon as they could prepare the necessary ID papers. They wanted me to start life anew as Paul Mangano, in South America, without my wife and child."

"But why?" I asked. "It doesn't make any sense."

"They wanted the authorities—and the world at large—to think I had died in the accident and that Paul Mangano had defected to South America. That way, the drug syndicate would have the DEA off their backs and could continue their trafficking unimpeded."

"You were willing to go along with such a scheme?" I challenged.

"Are you kidding? I protested loudly, until they threatened to kill Jackie and Stevie if I didn't coop-erate."

David tapped his fingers on the sofa cushion. "Then they didn't suspect you had gone over to Mangano's side?"

"They may have suspected," replied Steve, "but they didn't know for sure until last Wednesday at Meadowgreen Airport when Royce realized I had Paul Mangano's key, the key they had tried desper-ately to find. I cinched matters by slipping the key to you, Michelle, instead of turning it over to Royce or the Seward brothers."

"But you're here now," I argued, "apparently still an accepted member of the drug ring."

Steve scowled. "You don't get it, do you? I'm as much a prisoner as you are. They've held me here since I gave you the key, even forced me to forge Jackie's signature on funeral documents. These are

big-time criminals, Michelle. They play rough. Believe me, the Seward brothers still intend to bury
me—in fact, all of us."

David stood up and looked around. "There has to
be some way out."

"I've looked," said Steve. "I haven't found a
way to escape, but I did discover a stash of coke
in the belly of that mounted swordfish. I got a
feeling Royce is double-dealing the big boss."

"Our only chance is to radio the Coast Guard,"
David acknowledged, "if we can get past Andy
and the two crewmen before Royce gets back."

"I—I'm no good in combat," I stammered.

Steve looked at David. "Then it's two of us against
three of them."

David nodded. "I'm willing to take those odds."

"I have an idea," said Steve. "Get ready." He led
David to the stairwell. The two spoke quietly. Then
Steve shouted up, "Skipper, help! My son can't
breathe!" When there was no response, Steve
shouted again. "Come on, Andy! The boy's having
an asthma attack!"

Finally we heard Andy's heavy boots crossing the
deck and clambering down the stairs. As he reached
the last step, David tripped him. Andy fell forward,
sprawling awkwardly. Steve pounced, swinging.
David took the crewman that followed, hitting him
square on the jaw. The man reeled, stunned, then
came back fighting. A wild scuffle ensued. Steve and
Andy rolled against the wet bar, arms and legs
flailing.

I jumped out of the way as the crewman sent David
crashing into the coffee table. David scrambled to
his feet, blood spurting from his mouth. He deliv-
ered a solid punch to the man's temple.

Even as I ran to the galley and grabbed an iron pot, I could hear footsteps pounding on the deck above. Rotten timing! Royce was apparently back— with reinforcements. Trembling, I turned to confront them, my weapon poised over my head. But I gasped in amazement and relief as a brawny, bullish figure filled the stairwell. Clarence Harvey, the witty, madcap proprietor of Meadowgreen Airport, had come to our rescue!

CHAPTER
SEVENTEEN

If for one foolish moment I suspected Clarence Harvey of being our rescuer, my illusions were immediately shattered. As a revolver flashed in his grease-ingrained fist, Clarence barked, "What do ya know! We got us some unexpected guests on my little vessel."

The fighting stopped abruptly. Shock registered in David's face—and Steve's. Andy and the crewman swiftly pulled themselves to attention. Royce stepped forward beside Clarence.

"It can't be!" I cried. "You, Mr. Harvey! You're the one—!"

He ignored me. "Pull anchor, Andy, my boy. Set to sea."

"You making the run with us, sir?"

"I gotta take care of a few minor complications," he replied, nodding at David and me. Clarence looked out of character in an expensive sport shirt, denim deck slacks, and a captain's cap. His beady eyes narrowed under his scruffy brows as he taunted, "Well, Miss Merrill, Mr. Ballard, you two got yourselves a nasty habit of dropping in on folks out of the blue."

"We didn't drop in," I snapped. "We were brought at gunpoint."

I could hear the diesel engines gyrating as our Bertram 54 fishing vessel glided away from its floating dock. Moments later we passed Morro Rock. I felt a rolling, queasy sensation as we crossed the breakers and hit open sea. "Where are we going, Mr. Harvey?" I asked reproachfully.

He stepped forward, gesturing for David, Steve, and me to sit down on the sofa. "The *Wild Goose Chase* has a little meeting scheduled 200 miles at sea, Miss Merrill—one our friend Paul Mangano almost foiled. But don't you fret yourselves none. You won't be attending." He massaged his fleshy jowls, gloating with a ruthless cynicism. "We got another boatride planned for you—a one-way trip on a rubber raft in the icy waters of the Pacific."

Steve sprang from the sofa. "You can't get away with this, Clarence! These people are innocent. And I swear to God, I'll kill you if you lay one finger on my son!"

With his thin-lipped smile in place, Clarence shoved Steve back against the couch. "I don't listen to no traitors, Mr. Turman. I...eliminate them."

"Like you did Paul Mangano?" charged David.

"Sure enough. I figured I had a nice little switch game going until you and Miss Merrill blundered into my airport that day. Even so, my plans woulda gone A-okay, except for our turncoat Turman."

David nudged Steve. "I thought you didn't know who the mastermind was behind this drug operation."

"I didn't," Steve declared. "I pegged Clarence for a harmless buffoon. He ran that rinky-dink airport, that's all. I never took him seriously."

David wiped blood from his swollen lower lip. "Looks like he's used his folksy, down-home image to make us all play right into his hands."

"Cut the chatter, folks," ordered Clarence, lapsing into his cantankerous twang. He turned to Royce. "Watch 'em while I mosey on up to the bridge."

After Clarence had lumbered out, David slipped his arm around me and held me close. "You're trembling, Michelle."

"I feel the way I did after we crash-landed at Meadowgreen," I whispered. I ran my fingertips over David's wounds, from his puffy eyelid to his swollen lip. There was a large bruise over his left cheekbone. "My poor darling, you're hurt. Are we ever going to get out of this alive?"

"I'm okay, Sweetheart. No matter how things look, God is still in charge. We've got to hold on to that."

"But Clarence said he's going to throw us overboard," I cried. "David, I hardly know how to swim. And I'm seasick already!"

David almost smiled. "Joshua may get us out of this yet."

I laid my head on David's shoulder. "How I pray that he will."

Suddenly we heard a child's cry from the stateroom below. Little Stevie, pale and teary-eyed, scampered up the steps and dashed into his father's arms. "I don't feel good, Daddy," he whimpered, nestling against Steve's chest. "The boat's bumpy."

Steve clutched the boy as if he were afraid his son would be torn from his arms. Pressing his chin against Stevie's curls, he murmured in his smooth, deep voice, "It's okay, Son. Daddy's here."

As I witnessed Steve's unconcealed tenderness, my resentment against him began to dissolve. I yearned to gather little Stevie into my own arms, but I couldn't intrude on the warm camaraderie between father and son.

David reached over and gave Stevie an affectionate nudge. "Hi, Tiger. We tried to bring you your favorite duck, but we left him in the car."

"Don't remind him," I hissed.

"I want my goose," Stevie whined, looking up and rubbing his eye.

"We'll get it just as soon as we get back to shore," David assured him, giving me an abashed shrug.

I diverted Stevie's attention with a bright hello, adding, "We sure were worried. We looked and looked for you."

"Uncle Roys brought me to Daddy," he explained practically. He waved a stubby hand at Royce in the galley. "Uncle Roys, take Daddy and me to Mommy. We go home now."

Royce came over and handed Stevie a cookie. For the first time I saw tenderness in his expression. "I wish I could take you home right now, Kiddo. But it's out of my hands."

"It doesn't have to be, Royce," said Steve. "You and I could handle Clarence."

"Can it, Turman," snapped Royce, all gruffness again. "This is the big run. Nothing stops it. Besides, you got yourself into hot water. Don't come crying to me now."

"You care about Stevie—I know you do," Steve countered. "He's only three. He's no threat to you. You could convince Clarence to set him free...let the police find him and take him home to his mother."

"Please do as Steve says," I joined in plaintively. "The child's never done anything to you."

Royce gave me a withering glance. "He's the only one." He turned, strode to the wet bar, and poured himself a drink.

For the next half-hour we sat in subdued silence as the *Wild Goose Chase* plowed through an avalanche of waves, heading for its illicit rendezvous with a South American tramp steamer. At last I broke the silence with, "How fast are we going, Steve?"

"About 15 knots due west."

I nodded mechanically. I had no idea how fast that was. "Do you suppose we could persuade Clarence to put us aboard the tramp steamer instead of his rubber raft?" I ventured.

Steve shook his head. "Not a chance. Besides, with the steamer's foreign, hodgepodge crew and millions of dollars in illegal cargo, I doubt they'd welcome us with open arms."

We fell silent again, until an ear-splitting shout broke from the ship's bridge—Andy warning Clarence, "The *Cape Hedge* is heading our way!"

David pushed back the drapes over the sofa. We

stared out the expansive window. "It's the Coast Guard patrol boat," Steve said exultantly.

My hopes soared as I watched the gleaming white vessel in steady pursuit, several crewmen dotting the bridge, its mast silhouetted against a salmon-pink sky.

Within moments Clarence burst in the door, puffing, sweat beading on his forehead. I half-expected him to produce his red grease rag, mop his brow, and deliver a humorous aside in his cornpone drawl. But Clarence's eyes narrowed shrewdly as he announced, "Another minor complication, folks. Just a little flapdoodle. Nothing to be alarmed about."

"Are you kidding?" declared Royce, drawing his revolver. "The Coast Guard could throw a monkey wrench in all our plans."

"Put away your gun, Royce. We're clean," returned Clarence. "We ain't made our pickup yet. The Coast Guard is likely doing a routine check for code violations."

Royce eyed us. "What about them?"

"Take 'em below deck. Gag and tie them. Don't let 'em out of your sight." He rubbed his double chin methodically. "On second thought, leave Miss Merrill here with me. She's got a clean-scrubbed, Polyanna look about her. I believe I'll introduce her as my sweet little niece."

Royce looked skeptical. "You crazy, sir?"

"Crazy as a fox," Clarence smirked. "This young lady will make our little fishing expedition look downright virtuous."

I stared at Clarence, horrified. "Do you actually expect me to pretend I'm your niece?"

"Why not, Miss Merrill?" Clarence countered in his unruffled tone. "You keep in mind, one wrong move spells death for the boy. That goes for you fellas too," he told David and Steve.

I looked helplessly at David as Royce urged the three of them toward the stairwell. David mouthed the words *I love you* just before he disappeared below deck.

"The Coast Guard motor launch has left the cutter, sir," called Andy. "It's approaching our starboard side. Three crewmen aboard."

In his typically exuberant manner, Clarence opened the door and greeted the three Coast Guard crewmen with, "Howdy, folks. I'm Clarence Harvey, at your service."

My heart began hammering excitedly as the last man entered the deckhouse. There stood Joshua Kendrick in a navy-blue uniform and visor cap, carrying a baton and .45 automatic, handcuffs and flashlight on his utility belt. He gave me a knowing glance, as if to say, *Keep still. I'll work this out.*

"Routine safety and documentation inspection, sir," announced the tall, sandy-haired Guardsman, who wore a headset with mouthpiece.

Clarence nodded cockily. "Help yourselves, gentlemen. We're up to snuff. Your Report of Boarding will show her clean as a whistle."

I forced myself to remain nonchalant as Clarence slipped his arm around my waist and said, "This here is my niece, Michelle Harvey. She's trying her hand at a little sport fishing."

"If I can just manage to settle my queasy stomach," I said shakily, easing out of Clarence's grip.

"We just have a few questions, sir," continued the Guardsman, all business as he jotted something on an official form. "We need your vessel number, make, model, net tons—"

"Certainly," said Clarence. "Andy Watson's our skipper. He'll give you all the information you need."

Several minutes later, after the Coast Guard crewmen had completed their Report of Boarding and given the vessel a cursory examination, Joshua turned to me and extended his hand. With a wink that told me to play along, he said, "Goodbye, Miss Harvey. Thank you for allowing this interruption." He paused. "By the way, how has the fishing been?"

My mind raced. *Oh, God, help me to say the right thing!* Even as I prayed, I remembered something Steve had mentioned earlier. I walked over and patted the sailfish on the wall. "This is the type of catch we're after," I said meaningfully. "Uncle Clarence caught it, of course, but someone else stuffed it."

"A stuffed fish?" echoed Joshua, striding over.

"Loaded," I murmured.

Clarence stepped between Joshua and me and stroked the fish with undisguised pride. "Caught this beauty in Cabo San Lucas. They did a mighty fine taxidermy job on her too."

"Mind if I take a look at her myself?" queried Joshua.

"Suit yourself, but you ain't seen better workmanship nowhere."

Joshua ran his broad hand from the fish's sleek belly to its open, pointed jaw. Gingerly he felt inside. Then, with an effortless thrust, he brushed a fine white powder into his palm. "Cocaine, Mr. Harvey," he said.

"That's poppycock!" Clarence bellowed. "There's no cocaine on my vessel!"

"See for yourself." As Joshua reached inside the

fish's mouth and produced a small, telltale plastic bag, Clarence's face swelled with a purple rage. His eyes bulged virulently from their red-rimmed sockets.

"What nincompoop pulled this! Where's the double-crosser?" he thundered. "Royce Adams, get your tail up here!"

Immediately the sandy-haired Guardsman stepped forward, his revolver drawn. "Hold it, Mr. Harvey. You're under arrest."

Suddenly everything happened at once. Royce entered the deckhouse in response to Clarence's call. Joshua and the other Guardsman cut him off before Royce could fire his weapon. But with everyone's attention on Royce, Clarence yanked me against his bulky frame like a shield. I felt cold metal—the barrel of a gun—against my throat. He twisted my arm against my shoulder blade until I winced with pain. "Stop in your tracks, folks," he demanded. "One false move and this little lady gets blown right off this earth."

Joshua and the Guardsmen froze. Royce stepped forward, but Clarence waved him back. "You stashed the coke in my fish, didn't you, boy? Figured you'd make your own little deal on the side. You're the only buzzard greedy enough to do it, Royce. Blazes, you about wrecked our biggest run, the whole kit and caboodle!"

"Come off it, Harvey," groused Royce. "I've done your flying for you, taken all the risks, covered for you, been your flunky. You owe me plenty."

"We'll settle this later, fella." Clarence tightened his grip and turned me toward the sandy-haired Guardsman. "Hey, you there with your radio mike. Tell your lieutenant to back off. Get that cutter heading for shore. The *Wild Goose Chase* has a little powwow planned at sea. Don't matter how many uninvited guests we take along."

"Hear that, Lieutenant?" the Guardsman spoke into his microphone. "Better do as he says. He's taken the lady hostage."

"You'll never make it, Harvey," Joshua cautioned. "The reserves are behind you!"

Clarence laughed. "You can't fool me with that old trick—"

Before he could finish, David and Steve lunged from the stairwell, took a flying leap and tackled Clarence broadside. The impact threw me forward across the glass coffee table. I screamed as Clarence's massive hulk careened past me against the dining bar. His gun discharged in flight, blasting a hole in his prized sailfish. As Clarence sank to the floor, dazed, white powder trickled from the ruptured trophy onto his mussed salt-and-pepper hair.

"Bull's-eye, Harvey!" Joshua said triumphantly, retrieving Clarence's gun.

"We've taken charge, Lieutenant," the Guardsman said into his mouthpiece.

David sprang to my side and gathered me into his arms. I collapsed against him in relief as a warning voice exploded from the *Cape Hedge* bullhorn, demanding immediate surrender of the *Wild Goose Chase*.

• • •

An hour later we were aboard the *Cape Hedge* on our way back to Morro Bay. The 95-foot Coast Guard cutter cut a foamy pathway through pounding waves with the confiscated *Wild Goose Chase* in tow.

I felt queasy after the wave-dipping ride in the hard-bottomed Coast Guard boarding boat that transferred us from the *Wild Goose Chase* to the *Cape Hedge*. The officer in charge offered me a stool in the corner of the bridge. David helped me up, then stood close, his arm protectively around my waist. Joshua leaned against the doorway, his jaw set, his gaze intent.

The cutter's bridge was a compact area, the communications and control center of the ship. From our corner we looked down on the bow of the ship with a wide-angle view of the sea. The lieutenant JG stood by the coxswain chair, binoculars in hand, studying the sea. He spoke quietly to the serious-faced quartermaster at the helm, then turned to Joshua. "They've picked up the Seward brothers, sir, as you instructed."

"Any report on Meadowgreen Airport?" Josh asked.

"The FBI and your own agency are already en route there, sir."

David was suddenly alert. "What about my Bonanza? I left it at Meadowgreen for repairs."

Joshua gave David a crooked grin. "Sorry, Ballard. We won't be able to release your plane until we've made a thorough search of the airfield."

I put a restraining hand on David's arm. "But he will get the plane back, won't he, Joshua?"

"Of course." Josh turned his attention momentarily to the commanding officer. "Lieutenant, could you put a radio dispatch through to Sierra Vista Hospital? We need to let Mrs. Turman know her husband and son are both well and safe."

The lieutenant nodded. As the radio message went out, I looked toward the open deck, where Clarence,

Royce, and Andy were shackled to the iron railing. Steve was close by, embracing his son, murmuring paternal endearments that would have to last Stevie Jr. through the long months ahead.

"Josh, what about Steve?" I asked. "What will happen to him?"

Joshua tapped the Paul Mangano report retrieved from Clarence Harvey. "Paul made it clear Turman wanted out and was willing to turn state's evidence against the others. Fortunately, he had already taken steps in the right direction even before he realized Mangano was DEA."

"And what about Mr. Mangano?" I hesitated. "His family—do they know?"

I almost cried out at the pained expression on Joshua's face. "I talked to Paul's wife." There was a catch in his deep voice. "I'll be accompanying Paul's body back to Iowa. His wife wanted it that way." Josh looked away briefly. When he turned back to David and me, he was in control again.

"Do you think the courts will go easy on Steve?" David asked.

"Why should they?" Josh shot back. "Turman did deal in narcotics."

"But he did risk his life for Michelle and me."

"And himself." Joshua's voice was harsh. He looked again at the Mangano report. "But I'll do what I can..."

"What will happen to Clarence? And Royce?" I asked.

"We trust the courts will give them just what they deserve."

Even now as I glanced over at Clarence Harvey, I noted a vengeful glint in his eyes. "Clarence is only delayed, not defeated," I said.

"You're right," David agreed. "I suspect he's already plotting, maneuvering for the future."

Royce Adams was sullen-faced, handcuffed beside Clarence. "David," I said, "I almost feel sorry for Royce."

"Sorry?" David and Josh chorused.

"Yes. He's made so many wrong choices in life."

David nodded. "But he made one right choice for us below deck. He didn't tie up Steve and me the way Clarence ordered."

"He didn't? Why not?"

"I guess every man has a vulnerable spot," said David. "With Royce, it was Stevie Jr. When Stevie started crying and begged Uncle Roys not to tie up his Daddy, Royce gave in."

Joshua's brow arched. "So that's how you came to our rescue so quickly."

"That's it," David told him.

Impulsively I reached out and touched Joshua's hand. "Josh, we're so grateful you found us."

"Thanks to you, Michelle, and the clues you left in the phone booth at the post office."

"Actually I left the papers and my writer's notebook accidently. I forgot everything when Royce ordered me from the booth at gunpoint."

"Regardless, that page from the Mangano report listing the *Wild Goose Chase* led us to you just in time."

We fell silent. Josh didn't speak again until the *Cape Hedge* eased toward the Coast Guard dock at Morro Bay. As the boatswain gave the orders to secure the ship, Joshua extended his hand to David and me. "I appreciate you both for all your help. I'm not sure you realize the enormity of what's happened here. We're on the verge of breaking open one of the largest cocaine operations on the West Coast...thanks, in large part, to the two of you."

"To be honest, we had no idea what we were doing," I replied.

"Thank God, it turned out all right," said David.

Joshua clasped my hand a moment longer, then said to David, "When we dock, I'll have my men drive you to the post office for your car."

"Thanks," David answered.

I looked up at Joshua. "You will keep in touch, Josh? We'd like that."

He nodded. "I'd like that too, Michelle."

CHAPTER EIGHTEEN

In the two weeks that followed our return from Morro Bay, David and I settled back into our separate routines almost as if nothing had happened. He was once again the efficient, businesslike employer; I rejoined the ranks of hurried, overworked secretaries. Secretly I began to wonder if those days at Morro Bay had ever taken place. Were they merely a gossamer illusion of my writer's mind—half-dream, half-nightmare?

At unexpected moments—while watching a sunset or a love story on TV—I would feel a sudden yearning for David's arms, his kiss. I would think of things I simply had to tell him . . . but he wasn't there. At night I would awaken, terrified, with visions of Clarence Harvey or Royce Adams pursuing me. How I longed for David's comfort, his gentle voice assuring me I was safe!

Our Morro Bay trip had put David behind in his work. He had meetings to reschedule, trips to make, and several clients' ruffled feathers to smooth. I caught glimpses of him as he rushed in and out. We waved and exchanged helpless shrugs, and once he mouthed the words, *I'll catch you real soon!*

Would he? Did he even want to? Did our time together at Morro Bay mean as much to him as it did to me? Against all my plans and resolutions, I had fallen in love with David Ballard. He had said he loved me too. But had he spoken out of momentary passion . . . or enduring devotion?

Once, when Eva saw me gazing wistfully at David, she confided, "Give him time, Michelle. He has to feel he's back on top of things here at the office before he can concentrate on his personal life."

I tried to take comfort in her words. But inwardly I feared that what David and I had found so special together in Morro Bay might never be recaptured here at home.

On Tuesday morning I realized I would soon have a chance to test my suspicions. David stopped me by the water cooler and said, "How about a quick lunch in the cafeteria? I hear their tuna salad is the best this side of Monterey."

I laughed. "It's not half-bad if you wash it down with a tall lemonade."

"What are we waiting for?"

As David and I gingerly inspected our tuna specials, we talked about our Morro Bay odyssey.

"Have you got your plane back yet?" I asked.

"Yes. A few days ago," said David. "You know, of course, the DEA discovered that Meadowgreen Airport was a major hub for West Coast drug dealing. Clarence smuggled cocaine in on his fishing vessel, then flew the stuff all over the country."

I shook my head soberly. "I hope the courts make sure he never operates again."

"Steve Turman's testimony will help put Clarence and his cronies away for a long time."

"Speaking of Steve, I talked to Jackie last night. Their lawyer says Steve should get a reduced sentence for turning state's evidence."

"How is Jackie taking all this?"

"Better than I expected. She's so grateful Steve is alive. It helped, too, to know he was trying to get out of the mob and assist the DEA. She says she and Stevie will wait for him with open arms."

"Still, it won't be an easy wait," remarked David.

"No, but she won't be alone. Since Steve's arrest, she's reconciled with her parents—a miracle in itself. I plan to spend a lot of time with Jackie too. I want to share with her the peace I've found since making things right with God."

David nodded approvingly. "I'd like to follow up on Steve too. I figure he could use a friend right now."

"That would be wonderful, David. He needs to know what God can do in his life."

After lunch David walked me back to the office. He paused at my desk, looking earnest, almost boyish. "Say, Michelle, I promised you a night out to make up for the dinner show you missed at Sebastian's, remember?"

"Of course I remember." How could I forget?

"Are you free Friday night?" he asked. "I'll make it worth your while. And I guarantee, no more char-burned steaks."

I smiled. "If that's a promise, of course I'm free, David. What time?"

"Can you be ready an hour before sunset?"

I nodded, puzzled. "Where are we going?"

His eyes twinkled. "Somewhere fantastic, where you've never eaten before."

David wasn't exaggerating. On Friday evening, to my amazement, he picked me up in a shiny black limousine. We drove along Pacific Coast Highway to Laguna Beach and stopped by a deserted bluff overlooking the ocean. "Where's the restaurant?" I asked.

"Not far. I thought we'd take a walk along the beach first."

I glanced dubiously at my expensive Paris green chiffon dress and shrugged. "Oh, why not?"

We removed our shoes and ran like frolicking children down the rocky slope to the water's edge. Raptly we strolled arm-in-arm over the wet, packed sand. With David beside me, the world seemed transformed into a twilight paradise touched by enchantment. Gulls sang over our heads; the surf raged, spewing froth and foam; the chill, salty breeze raised goosebumps on my bare arms.

Or was it David's closeness that sent shivers through me? We talked like casual, longtime friends, but I could think only of how his lips would taste, how his arms would feel around me.

"Are you cold, Michelle?" David asked, rubbing my clammy arm.

"A little. My shawl's in the car."

We climbed the bluff again and returned to the

limousine. David retrieved my shawl, then ushered me away from the automobile. I looked at him, perplexed. "Aren't we going to the restaurant now?"

He smiled slyly. "Indeed we are."

For several minutes we walked along a boulder-strewn cliff jutting over a sapphire sea. By now my curiosity knew no bounds, but I was too stubborn to bombard David with senseless questions. Then I spotted it in a grassy haven, a lovely, incongruous sight—a candlelit table for two set with linen, crystal, and silver, silhouetted against a flaming sunset. Was it a mirage? A surrealistic apparition from a Salvador Dali painting?

"Oh, Shakespeare!" I exclaimed under my breath. "It's incredible!"

David led me over to the solitary little table and pulled back a chair. I drew back in protest. "No, David, we're intruding on someone."

"No, we're not," he smiled. "This is our party, Michelle. You're the guest of honor."

I sat down, too stunned to speak. A waiter in a crisp red jacket appeared and set a covered silver tray before me. He lifted the lid, revealing a steaming filet mignon, baked potato, and lobster on the half shell. With ease he poured two goblets of sparkling Perrier.

"Oh, David, how did you ever manage this?"

"Simple—with a little help from Eva and a catering service, and permission from the Parks and Recreation Department."

A violinist stepped from the shadows and began to serenade us. David caressed my hand. "I did this to show you how special you are to me, Sweetheart."

Tears brimmed in my eyes as I confessed, "I was

beginning to wonder if you still cared at all, David."

"I had to give us some breathing space, Michelle." He kissed my fingertips, one by one. "We needed time to think and pray. I wanted to be sure that what we have is real, lasting, deserving a permanent commitment."

"And—?" I held my breath.

"And I love you," he said simply. "I believe God has blessed what we've found together. In Morro Bay I was almost afraid to trust my feelings, my instincts. Now I know they were right on."

"I love you too, David," I murmured. "I never imagined I could feel this way."

David moved the candlesticks to one side and leaned across the table to kiss me. His lips were as sweet as I remembered, as warm as they had been in my dreams.